Good-Bye Russia, Hello America

GOOD-BYE RUSSIA,
Hello America

JANET S. KLEINMAN

GOOD-BYE RUSSIA, HELLO AMERICA

iUniverse books may be ordered through booksellers or by contacting:

iUniverse
1663 Liberty Drive
Bloomington, IN 47403
www.iuniverse.com
1-800-Authors (1-800-288-4677)

ISBN: 978-1-4917-6768-9 (sc)
ISBN: 978-1-4917-6767-2 (e)

Library of Congress Control Number: 2015909589

Print information available on the last page.

iUniverse rev. date: 08/06/2015

Author's Notes

Janet Kleinman, the child of immigrants, always wanted to acknowledge her family, who left Russia and came to America between the two world wars. That decision saved the next generation's lives.

The Sidowitzes thrived in America, but when the Second World War threatened to destroy their new land and the family they left behind, it was time to fight back, both on the home front and as soldiers who entered the labor camps of Europe and attempted to rescue the survivors.

And because of their courage and love of country, their family lives on.

Part 1

Chapter 1

Puffs of acrid white steam generated by the ship's engine belched and then rose up the smokestack of the *Lituania*, punctuating the clear blue sky on this wintry day at the port of Danzig on the Baltic Sea. Although the ship had been hosed down, the decks smelled of stale, rancid food and urine even before leaving the dock. Many of the passengers coughed, and others covered their noses with their hand-knitted scarves. It was a mob scene as families pushed and shoved to reach the rails and get a last look at the families they were leaving behind. They waved and shouted words of endearment that were drowned out by the sound of the smokestack as the ship set sail for America.

Jacov and Reuven Sidowitz stood on the rusting deck of the *Lituania*, an old steamship that plied the Atlantic, bringing immigrants to America. They smiled and waved good-bye to their eldest brother, Yehuda, who had driven them in his horse and carriage to the free city of Danzig, a seaport on the Baltic Sea. Wrapped in a heavy black coat, their mother, Ida, stood between them, tears of nostalgia mingling with tears of joy and streaming from her black eyes, emphasizing the determined look on her birdlike face.

"Yehuda, Yehuda!" she shouted as the *Lituania* departed. *"Cum zu America, schnell!"* (Come to America quickly). He was the only son from her first marriage to a dashing young writer and bookbinder who was killed by a Cossack's bullet when he refused to open his shop and service the soldier's needs on Shabbat. Ida and young Yehuda had hidden under the table in the back room behind the shop until the crashing of the storefront's glass subsided and neighbors came to help them.

A few years later, she married again. Velvel was a prosperous merchant who had one son, Lable, from his first wife, who had died in childbirth. She bore three more boys with Velvel—Natan, Reuven, and Jacov, the youngest—and raised all four boys with her precious Yehuda, the love-child of her first husband, as her own. But her brief happiness turned to grief when her second husband was killed in a horse-and-wagon accident as he returned from selling beets, carrots, and potatoes in his stall at the city market.

Now a widow, The Jewish Council permitted her to sell coal from house to house in the ghetto of the city. Ida barely eked out enough rubles to feed the six of them. She apprenticed the younger boys, Jacov and Reuven, as soon as they were eight to local boot makers, who were charmed by her tragic beauty. Refusing to obey the tsar's newest edict that required ten years of service in the Russian army or toil in a Siberian mine, the two older boys, Natan and Lable, ran away from Russia as soon as they could; one reached Belgium, the other the free city of Danzig. Then, separately, both stowed away on old, decrepit steamers and somehow reached America without getting caught, even though World War I had stopped immigration from Europe to America.

Ida had not seen the two runaways in five years, but mail and money arrived regularly. She saved every ruble she could for the upcoming journey to America. She was happy to be leaving the poverty of her homeland and eager to start a new life in America, surrounded by her four sons. The fifth might come eventually.

On February 3, in the frigid winter of 1923, the *Lituania* arrived in Boston without announcement or fanfare on the deck. Even the frigid Boston air could not disguise the smell of human sweat and stale urine that pervaded the boat. World War I, the war to end all wars, had ended, and thousands of Eastern Europeans were fleeing from the death and poverty that the war had left behind.

The crossing had been difficult. Babies died, and intestinal disease was rampant. Some unlucky travelers had contracted trachoma, an eye disease that was contagious and untreatable at that time, and they would be sent back to Europe after they docked.

Jacov and Reuven were strong young men, and Ida was a healthy woman. The three cleared immigration and were allowed to disembark. Like the trio, most of the immigrants clung together in family groups, looking for familiar faces—a brother, sister, or cousin who had generously sponsored their entry into the United States. They stood on the docks of Boston, light snow covering everything around them like a white blanket. Despite their shabby clothes and cheap suitcases, an air of excitement and anticipation echoed from the passengers, half a dozen languages emanating from the boisterous crowd.

Would they recognize Natan and Lable? Would their brothers recognize them?

When they left, Jacov and Reuven had been teenage boys. Now they were men, handsome men, and the young women on the ship had flirted with them to spice up the dreary voyage. Despite the shortage of water, the brothers managed to be clean shaven, and their wavy black hair shone against their olive skin. Their noses were straight, and their eyes were big and dark like the chunks of coal their mother had sold in the Jewish ghettoes of Brest to earn enough rubles to care for her children. Mama had aged but had remained beautiful.

On the collar of each of their jackets, immigration authorities had pinned a label. Their Hebrew/Russian name had been anglicized into Sidowitz. Jacov would become Jack, and Reuven would become Rubin. Mama Ida remained Ida.

They carried their papers and their brothers' letters in their pockets. To pass the time, Jacov, now Jack, took one out of his pocket.

"Listen," he read. "Lable and Natan are fixing radiators in Mr. Henry Ford's cars. Reuven—we should call you Rubin now—do you know who Mr. Ford is?"

"Don't know, but they must be earning many rubles. They sent us money every month until the war began. Then the letters stopped."

"Dollars, you mean. We changed them into rubles back in Brest."

"Dollars, rubles—it was money we needed."

"Funny, our brothers were tinsmiths back home. What do tinsmiths know about cars?"

"I don't know."

"They would never recognize Brest if they returned home. It is an ugly city now. The Poles, Germans, and Russians destroyed everything except the river."

Jack's voice cracked as he said, "But that's the land where we were born and where our papa is buried."

"But we are never going back," Rubin exclaimed.

Ida listened to her sons but said nothing. Except for her boys, the old country hadn't given her anything but grief.

"Why aren't they here yet?" said Rubin, pacing back and forth on the pier.

"Maybe they forgot that we were coming today."

"Schtill," Ida interrupted. "They'll come. *Meine yingeles*, my sons, will come for us."

The pier emptied. Families departed with their relatives. A few, like the Sidowitzes, waited impatiently. Ida sobbed softly.

Suddenly two full-grown men in tweed overcoats, their black hair neatly combed, pushed through the remaining immigrants and surrounded the waiting trio with their strong, sinewy arms, holding their family members at arm's length so they could see them better. Natan, unlike the others, had piercing, sky-blue eyes.

"Jacov, you didn't even shave when I last saw you."

"Reuven, remember your bar mitzvah, when you forgot the last words of your *parashah*? It was the day I hid on Uncle Hymie's roof until it grew dark. Then I scampered from roof to roof to where Mama and Yehuda were waiting on the outskirts of town. Mama kissed us good-bye, and Velvel drove us to Danzig. A woman in a big touring car stopped, said a few words to Louis. He helped her with her tons of crates, waved good-bye to me, and drove off with her to Belgium. I still don't know why. He never talks about his trip to America. I stowed away on an old freighter, and luckily I got to the United States. I might have wound up in Argentina. It was the last day I ever saw our family."

"Mama, Jacov, Reuven, let us look at you. We've missed you so much," said the oldest brother.

"I'm called Louis now, and Natan is now Nathan. Did they change your names too?"

"I'm Jack."

"I'm Rubin."

Everyone kissed each other. The men cried.

"Come," Louis said, and he picked up his mother's coarse sack of belongings. Nathan lifted his brothers' cheap cardboard suitcases. "We will be in New York tonight. Wait until you see our new car."

The new arrivals followed behind their kin until they reached the street and stopped at a late-model black Ford. Nathan took a gold-colored key out of his pocket. Louis put the luggage in the small trunk and opened the back door for his passengers.

Jack admired the Ford. "How many rubles do you need to buy such a car?"

"A *sach gelt*," Louis answered. "A lot of Yankee dollars, my brothers—not rubles. It takes *arbeit, arbeit, arbeit*—work, work, work. Nathan and I worked hard, and we saved money to send for you. We now own the gas station we worked in, and we are looking to buy another one. Together we can save enough to bring Yehuda and his family here in a few years."

"It would take less time if he came here now and worked and helped us save," Rubin said.

"I'm married," announced Nathan. "So I know why he doesn't want to leave his wife."

Jack and Rubin were delighted with the news. Ida did not respond to Nathan's announcement about his marriage. She was so overcome with joy at seeing her sons that nothing else mattered for the moment.

"*Meine kinder*, my children, I am so happy that we are all together again."

Rubin and Jack were hypnotized by the windshield wipers that swished the light snowflakes off the front window.

They admired the imposing buildings they passed until they reached a wider road, lit up by headlights that led to a highway.

The bumps were few. The journey was not as tumultuous as some of the nights at sea. The upholstered backseats were comfortable.

Ida's younger sons were awed and confused. In Brest they had had access only to a horse and wagon. They had seen few cars and had never ridden in one.

They hadn't been detained at Ellis Island either. Everyone in Brest knew about Ellis Island. Where had they arrived? Were their brothers finally taking them to Ellis Island? They were very tired. The next thing they remembered was reaching a place where a sign read Welcome to New York.

Chapter 2

Ida had finally fallen asleep. Jack peered out the right window, Rubin the left. Nathan and Louis took turns driving.

"The trees are like those in the Russian forests, tall, so very tall, and close together."

"They would be easy to hide in if the Cossacks come."

"Jack, this is America. There are no Cossacks here."

"What are those white lines on the road?"

Nathan answered drowsily. "They're called dividers. On one side of the line, a car goes one way; on the other side of the line, a car goes the other way. No one should get hurt in a crash."

"*Oy*, we have a lot to teach them," laughed Louis.

They glimpsed big farmhouses and barns, like the estates of the Russian landowners. The two younger brothers remained confused.

"Where is Ellis Island?" Rubin asked. "Are you taking us there?"

"No," laughed Nathan. "The steamship fare to Boston was much cheaper, and the inspectors aren't so strict. You passed your medical exams with flying colors. How do you like my English?"

"I don't understand. Were we ever in Boston?"

"For a few hours. It's a nice city, but wait till you get to New York. You've never seen so many big buildings, parks, and businesses. Many are owned by foreigners. It's a city where immigrants like us get rich."

"Rich? What do you mean by rich?"

Louis chimed in. "*Reich.* Enough to eat, a nice home, a car, a pretty girl. But first you need jobs. Remember Josef Levi? He's from Brest. In America, he's a foreman, an overseer, in a shoe factory. He can use a few smart operators. Mama, you were so smart to apprentice our brothers to Herschel, the boot maker. And thank goodness, boys, you shaved off your beards. The bosses don't want their workers looking like yids, Jews just off the boat, even though they are yids themselves. You'll have to become Yankees."

"My boys are good boys, like you and Natan. They are good boot makers. Too bad I could not send them to school to become doctors or *rebbes*."

Ida chose not to remember their anglicized names.

"It's okay, Mama. Here they will make a living, and their children will go to universities."

The boys fell asleep. Nathan, who had been driving most of the time, grew tired and exchanged places with Louis. The liquid in a gas gauge on the dashboard indicated that the gas tank was nearly empty.

"Louis, we need to stop for gas. If they wake up, we can eat the sandwiches that Sarah, my wife, packed before we left. And there are bathrooms on the station."

"Sounds good to me. I'm hungry. Look, just up ahead is a gas station."

After several pit stops and gas refills, the Sidowitz family drove through Westchester County and entered the Bronx. The sun had just risen.

Nathan turned west and wound up on the wrong side of the borough. They passed a cavernous construction site.

"Oy, what are they building?" queried·Rubin.

"The sign says '*Yenkee* Stadium—completion May 1921.' It's a place where grown up men vill play baseball.

"Don't they go to work?" asked Jack.

Louis and Nathan laughed and turned onto a gas station.

"In a few months, we'll take you out to the ball game. Sorry, we made a wrong turn. We know you're tired, but we need to fill up the gas tank one last time before we get you home."

Before one of the older brothers could get out of the car, go into the booth, and pay the man for gas, gun shots rang out. They saw a man who seemed dead lying on the cold station floor, surrounded by smashed bottles of liquor, their contents spilling out in all directions.

There was a pickup truck on the other side of the station, and two gorilla-sized guys were loading cartons into its back. Luckily, they were too busy to notice the black Ford parked on the side of the bathrooms.

Still naïve, Jack and Rubin screamed.

Nathan whirled around to the backseat and put his hands over their mouths.

"*Sie Schtill*! Be quiet. Don't move. They're *gengsters*. I think this station sells whiskey and vodka as well as gas."

"So?"

"It's against the law. You greenhorns know nothing. We are living under Prohibition."

"Prohibition?"

Louis softly explained the meaning of prohibition to his younger brothers. "Anyway, let's hope we have enough gas to get to the next station before the police get here."

"Is this the vilde west?" Mama chimed in.

"No, just *Italaynas-guineas* showing their muscle."

"Who?" asked Jack.

Before Louis or Nathan could answer, the sound of a police siren grew louder. Louis revved the engine and raced away from the station. The Irish policemen didn't like kikes any better than Italians.

It was almost dawn when Louis pulled up in front of 742 Brook Avenue in the East Bronx. Lighter snow than they had experienced in Russia had been shoveled up against the red brick building and against the curb. Nathan managed to park the car on a snow bank with the front of the Ford facing up, so it would be easier to back out into the street.

The building was six stories of red brick, like the others on the block. Each had a stoop that went directly to the second floor so the builders avoided the cost of putting in an elevator.

Nathan commented, "These buildings are called walk-ups. Your apartment is on the fourth floor."

The family got out of the car. Each member picked up a piece of luggage or a bag of groceries and followed Nathan on the long climb, like a file of tired soldiers following their officer to an unexplored destination.

"*Vere* are you taking us?" Mama asked. "Are we to live in heaven?"

"Don't worry, Mama. It'll be all right. You'll have nice neighbors."

In the building, they could hear a man and woman arguing in a strange language. Mama said it was Polish. A baby was crying, and a dog was barking.

"Move over, greenhorns," shouted a man carrying a wire basket of milk bottles as he rushed up the steps to make his deliveries.

On the fourth floor, they turned right and stopped at a

door that said 4G. Louis took a key out of his pocket; they all followed him into the four small rooms, dropping their luggage as they went. The apartment was sparsely furnished, but there were enough beds for the three newcomers. Nathan left a bag of rolls and a jar of jam in the kitchen for breakfast in the morning.

"Goodnight, Mama. Goodnight, Jacov and Reuven—I mean Jack and Rubin. We are going home. Get some sleep." Everybody kissed everybody. "*Sorg sach nicht*. Don't worry. Don't be scared. We'll be back in the morning."

Left alone in this strange apartment in the sky, in a new country, unsure of tomorrow, Jack, Rubin, and Mama Ida were speechless, and they began to unpack.

Chapter 3

unday morning, Nathan and Sarah, his pregnant wife, and Louis and Minna, his latest girlfriend from Romania, trudged up the steps of 742 Brook Avenue loaded with brown grocery bags.

Nathan knocked. "Ve're here," and he pushed the door open. "Put away the jelly," he shouted. "We have real food."

"Here, Mama," added Louis, handing her the Maxwell House can. "Put up the coffee. We're going to have a feast."

The ladies covered the crude kitchen table with a large blue bed sheet, found a few plates in the cabinets, and filled them with cuts of sturgeon, slices of lox, tomatoes, onions, and cucumber. They put the cream cheese on a butter dish that the former tenants had left in the fridge. They had brought along napkins and cutlery. A small straw basket they found in the living room became a receptacle for the bagels.

"So much food! You could feed the whole village on Shabbat," gasped Ida.

"What are those round rolls with holes?" asked Jack.

"Bagels, you dummy," said Nathan playfully, and he smacked his young brother's handsome head.

"Bagels," echoed Rubin. "How do we eat them?"

The others laughed. "Just watch us." And Nathan and Louis sliced the bagels in half, smeared them with cream cheese, and layered them with lox, tomato, and onion. They cut the sturgeon in small cubes to be savored as a special treat.

"Just like Russia—ha—where we were lucky to get brown bread and herring on Shabbat morning."

"Only *reiche menshen,* rich people, ate like this," said Mama. "Sometimes when it was freezing cold and I sold a lot of coal, I fried up a herring and baked a few potatoes in the fire. Papa, before he died, used to suck out the eyes and the inside of the head of the herring."

"Enjoy, enjoy, but let's get down to business. Rubin and Jack have an appointment with Josef Levi tomorrow morning. They need two new operators at the shoe factory."

"How do we get there?" asked Jack.

"Nathan will take you to Houston Street and show you how to use the subway."

"Subway?"

"Yes, the iron train that goes under the ground."

"I won't be able to stay with you all the time," Nathan added. "We have a lot of radiators to repair at the station. Have Josef write down everything you need to remember: what time you start working, when you stop, any tools you will need. Tell Josef that I'll take care of him at the poker game Thursday night."

"I brought my awl and leather scissors with me," said Rubin.

"Me too."

"Smart boys."

"How will we know how to come back home?" asked Jack.

"Don't worry. Watch how we get there. Then go down the same Houston Street subway station you came out of, but go to the Bronx, not Brooklyn. Half of the passengers speak Yiddish, so don't be ashamed to ask for help if you need it. I'll give you nickels so you can go through the turnstile and onto the train platform. Remember to get off at the Brook Avenue station."

While the men continued to talk, Sarah and Minna cleaned up the dishes. Ida kept staring at Sarah.

"Sarah, you look so familiar. Are you from Brest?"

"Yes, Ida. Nathan helped you deliver coal to my father's house."

"*Du bist* Michele, the wheat merchant's *tochter!* Tramp, you chased my Natan all over the *shtetl.*"

Sarah turned crimson. "I loved him since he was a little boy. You tried to keep him away from me. Yes, it's true; I even chased him to America."

"Has he married you?"

"With a ring and a rabbi and Louis as a witness. Can't you see my belly?"

Sarah burst into tears and dropped a plate. It broke into countless pieces. She ran into the bathroom, and her howls of distress could be heard all over the apartment. Minna, Louis's recent girlfriend cleaned up.

Nathan and Louis put on their coats and escorted the two women out of the house. As Louis marched them down the stairs, Nathan went back inside.

"Mama, never speak to Sara that way again, or you'll never see your grandchild. I told you I was married on the ride from Boston to New York. You weren't listening."

"You didn't tell me it was that *vilder chaya*, that wild animal."

"She's a good wife. Write her parents a letter and tell them how happy she is and that we are expecting a child. Louis and I will pick up the boys tomorrow morning. Meanwhile, the three of you go for a walk and see what the neighborhood looks like."

"You're the boss now, but you should know that I miss Yehuda most of all."

Seething with jealousy despite his affection for his older brother back in Russia, Nathan slammed the door and left the apartment.

Jack and Rubin arrived at the Brighton Boot Company in a downtown Manhattan loft without getting lost. Business was booming, and the two young men were hired on the spot and given a station next to the other operators. Except for the foreman, who was a tough first-generation American from Brownsville, all the operators chattered in Yiddish or Italian. It was almost a symphony of sound, with the zigzagging of the machines acting like an orchestra.

The men were young and handsome. Some were married; many were single. Their testosterone levels were high, and they viewed every pretty woman with longing.

Meanwhile Mama Ida adjusted to the neighborhood. She met the butcher, the baker, and the greengrocer. She stopped in at a variety store and bought pots and pans and cooking utensils. Almost all the shopkeepers spoke Yiddish. Angelo, the Italian shoe repairman, had a sign in his window reading Yiddish Spoken Here. Only the barber from Rome, who sang Caruso arias while he worked, refused to speak anything but classic Italian unless it was absolutely necessary.

On Friday nights, Ida covered the chipped wooden table with a clean white sheet. She set out the mismatched dishes that she had bought earlier in the day from the secondhand store at the end of the block to ensure that she had enough plates and soup bowls for her whole family. Then she covered her head with a lace kerchief, lit her great-grandmother's brass candles that she had brought with her all the way from Brest, and said her prayers. "Baruch atah Adonai …"

She had expected all her sons to be there for Erev Shabbat, but Louis and Nathan made excuses and didn't come. Jack and Rubin were growing ornery and had made arrangements to attend the burlesque theater on Third Avenue with some of their co-workers as soon as dinner was over.

Rubin recited the blessing over the challah and handed a piece of the Shabbat bread to each of them; Jack made kiddush, blessing the wine. Ignoring the empty places at the table, they ate Mama's roast chicken and garlic mashed potatoes while looking at their watches.

"Do you want dessert, my *boyes*?"

They didn't want to hurt her feelings.

"Okay, Mama, but we'll skip the tea. We've been invited to a party."

"A party on Erev Shabbat? Are you *goyem,* gentiles?"

"Mama, this is America."

"Who invited you? Except for your brothers, who do you know in New York?"

"Some of the workers in the factory come from Brest. The party is to welcome us to America."

Mama shrugged her shoulders. "*Geh,* go—be careful. I do not trust your new friends, the Italianas especially."

"Don't worry," Rubin added as he patted her head. "We'll go to shul with you in the morning."

"Today is Friday, so where are your paychecks? Don't take all your *gelt* (money) with you," she warned.

Each took a few dollars out of the envelopes the boss had given them and handed her the rest of their salaries.

Mama watched as the boys changed their shirts and shaved, brushed their thick, wavy black hair, and slapped on a little aftershave. She felt blessed to have such handsome, good sons.

"Tell me again, where are you going?"

"To the burlesque theater on Third Avenue."

"Burlesque? What is that?"

"Singing, dancing, *schone madlach*—pretty girls."

"*Nacavas*—whores," she hissed.

"Don't be silly, Mama."

Shaking a threatening finger at them, Ida issued one more warning. "Don't bring me home a *schickser*, either of you."

Jack and Rubin kissed Mama on her cheeks and ran out the door and down the four flights of steps.

Burlesque—they couldn't wait.

Ida smiled. She had once been young too.

Chapter 4

Ida couldn't sleep. Every step she heard in the hallway made her think that her sons were coming home from the burlesque theater, whatever and wherever that was. The clock on the night table next to her bed reminded her that it was already two in the morning.

Suddenly she heard the shuffling of feet ascending the creaky staircase. Then there was laughter, followed by voices. One voice was Jacov's, but the other voice was a high-pitched female's. Somewhere on the fourth floor, a door opened, but the pair that had ascended the stairs remained in the hallway.

She recognized the rustle of clothing being rearranged, and then the oohs and ahs of two bodies touching, perhaps even kissing, and moments later the exaltation of a climax. A door closed. There was silence.

"Rubin, you can come upstairs now."

"It's about time. I'm freezing."

"We better get inside before Mama wakes up."

"You sure didn't waste any time tonight, brother."

"Beatrice was as hot as me. She's beautiful, isn't she?"

"She sure can dance with that feathered fan! I was not as lucky as you tonight."

"You will be, little brother … maybe next Friday."

Ida pretended to sleep as Jack and Rubin unlocked the door to 4B, quickly disrobed, and got into their beds.

Oy veh, she thought. *Mrs. Silverman's daughter dances in front of men wearing a feather. How can my roast chicken compare with that? Where are the matchmakers in America? I'll pray they get over this nonsense in shul tomorrow morning.*

As the weeks went by, Ida grew more and more disappointed with her sons. They stopped reciting prayers and found excuses—a football game, working overtime, an old friend who just arrived from Russia—for not going to Shabbat services with her.

One Shabbat she met Morris Cohen, the president of the synagogue, at the kiddush following the service.

"May I carry your plate of lox and other goodies to the table for you?" he asked.

She was about to say that she could do it herself, but she restrained herself. Mr. Cohen was one of the men who wore an expensive *tallis* (prayer shawl).

"It would be my pleasure. Should I get the coffee?" Ida offered.

"Later, sometimes they set out urns—big coffee pots—on each table."

Before she and Morris could start a conversation, a young girl ran up to Mr. Cohen.

"Papa, Papa," she said. "There are two young men standing at the corner street of the shul smoking cigarettes. The shorter one said his name was Rubin, and he flirted with me. He has an accent just like yours."

Mr. Cohen ignored his daughter's unkind reference to his speech but commented on the two young men.

He shook his head in disgust as he muttered, "A *shanda*, a shame," to Ida.

Ida blushed. Could it be her son Rubin? *Why isn't he in shul instead of outside?*

"Mrs. Sidowitz, this is Rachel, my sweet *tochter*—daughter in English. So I'm a greenhorn, a foreigner … so what? Everyone in America started as a foreigner."

"How nice to meet you," Ida said. " I have two handsome sons."

"Are they here?"

"Not today."

"It's Shabbat. I hope they're not the ones smoking on the corner."

The following Friday, Louis reluctantly picked up his mother. They walked a few blocks to Nathan and Sarah's house for Erev Shabbat dinner. It was the first time Ida was there, and she was mesmerized by the elevator that carried her up to the sixth floor. Louis rang the bell. To Ida it sounded like the chimes of a church. Nathan opened the door; Ida took off her snow boots and peeked inside. She was awed by the finery of the apartment: the tufted velvet couch, the big dining room table with high-back chairs and elaborately designed jacquard cushions. The table was set with Depression glass dishes that Sarah had collected by going to the movies when Nathan worked late. But to Ida the dishes looked elegant.

"Nathan, close the door. The draft is cooling my chicken soup."

"Okay, okay, Sarah. I'm just letting Louis and Mama in."

"Where are Jack and Rubin?" Ida asked.

"They had other plans."

"You didn't tell me that your brothers weren't coming. Where were they going for Shabbat?"

"Pitkin Avenue," Louis chimed in.

"Where is Pitkin Avenue?"

"In Brooklyn. It's where the single greenhorns go to mingle after working in shops—factories—all week."

"So why aren't you there, Louis?

Before Louis could answer, Nathan came out of the kitchen carrying a tureen of chicken soup with *knadlach,* called matzo balls in English.

"To the table everyone. My Sarah is a great cook."

Sarah stood before the Shabbat candles and recited the blessing: "Baruch, atah Adonai …" Nathan sanctified the wine. Mama stood before the challah covered by an embroidered cloth. She thanked God in prayer for allowing the family to have food to eat.

Nathan ladled out the soup. Sarah, with her big belly, never glanced once at her mother-in-law.

Chapter 5

There was a knock at the door.

"Come in," Sarah yelled, annoyed by the interruption to her first formal Shabbat dinner.

A pretty, rather disheveled young woman pushed open the door.

"Oh, I'm sorry. I see that you have company. I'm Esther Marcus, Sarah and Nathan's neighbor. Sorry I'm not dressed for the Shabbat. My mama's mad at me. It was so busy at the florist's shop that I forgot to stop at Mr. Levy's grocery store on my way home from work and buy candles. Can you lend me two? I'll return them during the week."

Ida snapped, "You know you're late in lighting the candles."

"So …?" Louis said. "God will forgive her." He couldn't help noticing how pretty Esther was, with her flashing brown eyes and dimples on either side of her mouth.

Sarah arose from her chair and limped into the kitchen. It was becoming difficult for her to walk.

Louis's gaze took in Esther's shapely legs. The guys at the station called him a leg-man.

"What's keeping you?" Nathan called when Sarah didn't return. "We're all hungry. Where are the roast chickens?"

Sarah screamed, "I'm standing in a puddle of water. I'm peeing in my pants. Help, I don't know what to do!"

Esther Marcus forgot about the candles she had come to borrow. Mama cleared and cleaned off the table to avoid roaches. Louis forgot about the roast chickens and made sure that the stove was turned off and then went for the car.

In the bedroom, Nathan found the small suitcase Sarah had prepared just for this moment. He helped his wife remove her wet underwear as the pains started, and he slipped her into an oversized terry cloth bathrobe. Nathan and Esther helped her to the elevator.

Louis was waiting in front of the tenement. It was only a short ride to the hospital.

For over two hours, Sarah moaned her way through the delivery. A seven-pound, eight-ounce healthy baby boy entered the world and made his presence known by crying.

Nathan was ecstatic. He kissed his wife, took a box of cigars out of Sarah's suitcase, and gave them out to his brother, the doctors, and any other male he saw on the hospital floor.

A nurse entered the room carrying an official-looking folder. "Congratulations. You have a lovely son. What do you want to name him?"

There were lots of American names that Nathan and Sarah liked, but he knew they'd have to name him William or Ida would be mad at them forever. She had worshiped her late husband, who had been killed in a pogrom twenty years before. Nathan hardly remembered him, but so what. He and Sarah now had an American son, a citizen of the United States of America, a first in the Sidowitz family.

"Miss Kingsley—is that what your tag says?

"Yes."

"Ve vish to call him Velvel—William in English."

The affair between Louis and Esther grew intense. He was spending a lot of time pretending to be uncle to the children of his neighbors so he could bump into Esther in the hallways of the building on Brook Avenue. Esther, with her shapely legs, didn't push him away when he leaned her against a hallway wall and stole a kiss, or more. The lovers were oblivious to the savory smells, the crying children, and the domestic arguing that characterized buildings overstuffed with extended families. Esther had bewitched him.

And despite Ida's endless urging, Louis refused to meet the synagogue president's daughter.

Esther had come to America as a child; she'd learned bookkeeping at high school and wanted to marry a doctor. She worked in the office of a hardware company and made a good salary. But she was now twenty-seven, and no doctor had wanted to marry her.

Louis wasn't bad-looking and had a good business. So what if he fixed automobiles instead of bodies and came home a little greasy? He scrubbed himself clean before fondling her. The relationship became serious.

One night, they met at Feigy's Bagel Parlor for a light supper.

"Esther," Louis said as he reached across the table and took her hand. "How about moving in with me and Mama?"

"Are you crazy? What am I, a whore?"

"No, no, sweetheart, I didn't mean that! Will you marry me? I'll make you a good husband." Then he took a small engagement ring out of a silver box and slipped it on her finger.

Aware that she might be pregnant—she had found a torn condom outside her door one morning and now her period was late—Esther agreed.

"I think I love you, Louis, but your mother doesn't like me. Will it work out?"

Louis kissed her without further comment.

Two weeks later they had a simple ceremony at a rabbi's house. Esther wore a soft blue dress with lace trim; Louis wore his only suit, a navy blue wool blend that had been cleaned and pressed. They spent their honeymoon in Louis's bed pretending that Ida was not drinking tea and crunching a sugar cube in the kitchen half the night.

Esther and Mama quarreled constantly. Esther was a healthy young woman. She continued working at the hardware store, so she only saw Mama Ida at night. She wasn't sorry that she didn't have to cook. Finally, when her belly extended so that customers made remarks, her boss suggested that she quit her job. It was time to prepare for the birth of their baby.

One day she asked Ida, "How come you're not knitting a sweater for the baby? I see all the other grandmas knitting while they are sitting on the stoop."

"Learn to knit yourself. My fingers are too arthritic."

"Then will you teach me how to cook? Louis loves your stuffed cabbage and gefilte fish."

"You never learned how to cook? What kind of mother did you have?"

"She was busy working in a factory all the time. Papa left us when I was eight years old. Everything we ate was from the deli or just plain lettuce and tomato sandwiches."

"So, why should I teach you how to cook? This is my house, and I'll do the cooking around here. Louis loves my potato pancakes and my noodle pudding too."

Esther was startled at her mother-in-law's angry retort. She couldn't understand Ida's harsh reactions to her.

"Why should I let you watch me? It's enough you stole my

son from me, but you'll not get my recipes. It's not as if you were a princess, like the shul president's daughter."

Ida turned her back on Esther, spread her large white apron, and made it impossible for Esther to watch her chop, season, or cook.

Esther cried that night.

"Louis," she said, as she sidled up close to her husband. "After the baby is born, I want our own apartment."

"I can't leave my mother."

"Yes, you can. The younger boys are still at home."

"Hardly ever. They're out chasing skirts."

"They can take turns staying home a little. Maybe one of them is right for the shul president's daughter."

Ignoring her sarcasm, Louis tried to pull her closer to him in the bed, kiss away her anger, and make her forget. She pulled away from him.

"Louis, either she goes or I leave you after the baby is born. Of course, I'll take the baby with me."

"Please, Esther, be patient. I'll figure out what to do. I love you."

The following week, as night fell, a group of strike breakers—hoodlums brandishing bats—attacked the shoe workers as they came out of the building. Jack and Rubin fought back with their fists. There were bloody noses, torn clothes, black eyes, but no guns. The siren of a police car broke up the riot, and everybody scattered.

Rubin and Jack cleaned up at a nearby public bathhouse. Both were late for their end-of-the-workweek Friday-night frolic. Jack headed for the uptown subway with a wave to Rubin.

"See you at home later tonight."

"Where are you going, brother?"

"Uptown, to the garment center. Met an assistant designer the other day in the library, where they were giving English lessons. She wears short skirts and tight tops and has a small waist. Pretty little thing. Says she's a flapper, but I'm not sure what a flapper does."

"Flap, of course," Rubin joked.

"Don't be so funny, Rubin. She wants to be a noted dress designer some day." And he crossed the street and rushed off to the subway.

"Enjoy. I'm going down to the union hall," Rubin shouted after him.

Then he walked a block to the elevated trains going to Brooklyn. As he rushed up the stairs, he marveled at the underground trains, the locals and express subways. What a city he was in. It went everywhere and came back to where you started from in eight hours. He reached the train platform as a number seven was pulling into the station, and he boarded it before the doors closed. The signs on some of the windows of the car said Brownsville-Canarsie.

In a short time he arrived at the station nearest to Pitkin Avenue. It was later than usual, but still full of young factory workers celebrating the welcome end of the workweek. Rubin pushed his way through the crowd, hoping to catch a glimpse of Eslatka and her nephew Ben, but no luck. They were nowhere to be found.

It was a cold, windy winter night, and he was sorry that he hadn't taken his gloves. But he tied a woolen scarf around his neck and headed toward Herzl Street. No one was sitting on the stoop, so he entered the boarding house. There in the center of the broad entryway, on a bench next to a large wood-burning stove, sat Eslatka, tears gushing down her face.

He kneeled down beside her, took her hands in his, and said, "*Bist du* all right?"

"No, *Ich bin sehr kalt.*"

"Let me warm you up." He took off his woolen scarf and draped it around her neck.

Her tears continued to flow. "Who are you?" she said.

"I'm a friend of your cousin Benny. Come, we'll have a cup of tea, and you'll feel better."

Trembling, she let Rubin take her arm and lead her out the door. Downstairs under the stoop was a tiny restaurant with only three tables and a curtain on the window. It looked warm and welcoming.

Rubin ordered two cups of hot tea with lemon. They were served with sugar cubes in the saucer. She took a sip of the hot liquid. He bit into a sugar cube as Eslatka poured out her story. She had no parents, no protector, and no money. She earned only eight dollars a week and could hardly pay her rent. Sometimes she went without dinner. Her tears started flowing again.

Rubin handed her his handkerchief to wipe her tears. "Come back to the union hall with me. I'll find you a nice roommate and get someone to get you a union card. Monday we'll get you a job in a union shop. I know people. You'll earn more money and won't have to go hungry."

Eslatka was desperate. She was also naïve, and for some reason she would never understand when she thought about it months later, she trusted him. Rubin paid the bill, and the two hurried the few blocks to the union office. Daisy, the manager, was there, sitting on the lap of a union big shot, a delegate of the Ladies Garment Workers, who had a wife in Canarsie.

Rubin would remember that on Monday morning, and Eslatka would get her new job.

Chapter 6

World War I had interrupted the flow of immigrants to the United States and left a lot of the lonely bachelors already there unable to find a bride. A few years after the war ended, thousands of new immigrants—wives and families, unaccompanied single men, and single women—flooded the eastern cities of the United States.

Nathan had married before he brought his mother and brothers to America, and Louis soon after. Getting pregnant in the first few months of marriage was a badge of honor for the couple, fulfilling the new bride and making the groom feel ultra-macho every time he looked at her. It was as if having a child in this new land not long after arriving on US soil made the newcomers feel more secure about becoming citizens and being able to stay.

Both Louis's and Nathan's children were born at the end of the Roaring Twenties. Nathan's boy turned two; Louis's daughter was an adorable eight months. Business at the gas station was booming. More and more guys were getting married, starting families, and taking out loans to buy cars. And their radiators were always leaking.

Rubin and Jack were sowing their wild oats and looking

for round, well-shaped virgins, preferably from the Old World. With the economy soaring, the nation's women were buying shoes by the dozen, and shoe operators were working long hours to meet the demand. The brothers were working overtime, and their wages were good.

But working conditions were dismal. Buildings were unsafe; windows were locked, with no emergency exits. Many worked sixty hours a week. Lunch brought from home was eaten at the machine; bathroom breaks were often timed by a despotic overseer known as the foreman.

The workers grew increasingly dissatisfied. Piecework was seasonal and offered no benefits. They got paid according to how many pairs of shoes they produced. The pay was the same for sewing plain pumps as ornate sling-backs with fancy stitching and jeweled buckles. The employment rate fluctuated from month to month. Labor wanted fairer weekly wages and benefits, as well as better working conditions and some kind of job security. Unions began to form. Owners resisted. Periodically, strikers left their machines and took to the street. So did Jack and Rubin.

"Wages belong to the workers" became their slogan as pickets encircled factory buildings and police shoved the men around, often injuring them with their billy clubs. Rubin and Jack had less time for chasing skirts. The shoe workers union was in its infancy. The brothers spent hours organizing strategies to make their bosses more responsive to their demands. They shared the basement on Pitkin Avenue with the expanding Ladies Garment Workers Union that now included women.

One rainy Friday evening as Rubin dashed out of the office to get a frankfurter from the kosher deli on the corner, he saw her again, a petite girl with hazel eyes and a sweet mouth being walked up and down the avenue by a short, good-looking guy under a big umbrella. The couple stopped at a haberdashery shop, and the man spoke to a pair of men admiring the new suits in the window. His unaccented English made it apparent that he was no immigrant. The girl never uttered a word but smiled sweetly at the men he stopped to chat with.

"Hey, Daisy, who's the girl with that sharp American-looking guy?" Rubin asked a seamstress he knew who was also walking out of the union building.

"You mean Eslatka? Just got here from some *shtetl* in Poland. The nuns rescued her from a Russian Cossack and taught her how to sew. There were no relatives to care for her, so an organization called HIAS brought her over on an orphans' ship. Speaks no English, but she has golden hands. Her nephew Benny wants to get her into the union."

"Her nephew?"

"Yeah, her nephew's father is her brother. It's a long story, but the old man got her into America with a little pull from the Sanitation Workers Union. He didn't want to be a *schneider*—a tailor, you know—so he collects garbage for a living and makes more money working with the Italians."

"And the man?"

"He's a winner. No dirty factory work for him. Came here young enough to go to high school, and maybe even a little college. I think he sells insurance for a living. Benny gets a kick out of parading his pretty aunt up and down the avenue to frustrate you greenhorns. She's a looker, isn't she? Want me to introduce you?"

"No. I've met her already. Just wanted to know more about her."

Rubin finished his frankfurter, wiped the mustard from his mouth, and watched the Friday-night thrill seekers eyeing Eslatka. He followed the pair. At a stoop on Herzl Street, Benny kissed his aunt on the cheek, said a few words to her in Yiddish, and left her going up and into Mrs. Bloom's rooming house.

Rubin smiled and thought to himself, *I'll know where to find her when I'm ready.*

Chapter 7

Meanwhile, uptown, Bela sought refuge from the cold in the lobby of a deco-styled combined office/factory building on West Thirty-Seventh Street, just a block off Seventh Avenue. It was the heart of the garment center, but it was deserted after seven in the evening. Most of the workers had scattered to the outer boroughs where they lived and where candles were being lit before Friday-night dinners were served. The empty rolling dress racks were lined up in the alleys separating some of the brown brick buildings. Monday morning they would start crossing the streets from factories to showrooms, blocking traffic.

Jack knocked on the glass door. Bela waved a gloved hand at the security guard and he let her out of the building. Instinctively, Jack encircled her with his arms and then pulled back.

"Sorry, am I being too fresh? I kept seeing you at every station platform from Houston Street to Thirty-Fourth Street."

"No, I like a guy who acts on his impulses."

"Impulses? Does that mean I can kiss you if I choose to?"

"Don't be a silly," she said. Then she grasped his hand and led him to the biggest cafeteria he had ever seen. Rows of glass-covered shelves enclosed in brass contained everything from tuna sandwiches to hot corn to dishes of baked beans. Next to each dish was a slot for nickels. You slipped in the number of nickels called for, pulled a lever, and a glass door opened. Your dinner or dessert was there for the taking. Jack was awed. There was nothing like this restaurant on Houston Street.

"It's magic!" he exclaimed.

Bela smiled at him. "It's called an automat."

"What if you don't have nickels?"

"See that cashier over there?" She pointed to a lady in a glass-enclosed booth. "If you don't have nickels she'll change your bills. She also supplies brass coins if you want to buy more expensive items at the steam table."

Bela introduced Jack to macaroni and cheese. He loved putting the coins in the slots and watching the revolving shelves deliver the food. They got silverware and napkins from a stationary server, and found a table near the window looking over Seventh Avenue. Everyone was eating, laughing, and telling jokes. Suddenly Jack turned to Bela. "I like this kind of life. Will you marry me?"

"Are you crazy?"

"Yes, I'm crazy about you."

"Will you go into business with me? I'll design and sew. You'll sell, Jack."

"We might make a good pair."

"So you'll go into business with me?"

"I will if you marry me. I'll get my brother Nathan to lend us his car and we'll elope to Maryland. I hear that you can get a license and get married on the same day. Maybe we'll take Rubin and his secret girlfriend along with us."

"But you haven't even met her."

"Rubin talks in his sleep. Imagine, her name's Eslatka, and he's in love."

"*Du bist mishuga*, (you are crazy), but you're so handsome."

Jack leaned across the table and kissed her.

When they finished eating, Bela took Jack to a small café for coffee. There they were singing Russian songs. Nutcrackers and bowls of walnuts were on each table. Everyone was cracking shells to reach the sweetmeats, talking and chewing. A few romantic couples danced close to one another. Bela and Jack preferred to dance.

"Bela, let's go find my brother in Brooklyn. I know where he hangs out. If he wasn't a year older than me, you'd think we were twins. On the boat coming to America we talked about meeting two nice girls and having a double wedding. I think Eslatka lives in Brownsville."

"Why is it so important that we get together?"

"We're a close family. And I hear she's a great dressmaker—you're a designer. Maybe we're a fit. Rubin could be the inside man and run the factory. I would go on the road, weekdays only, I promise you, to sell your dresses."

Bela laughed. "Okay, let's try it. Four of us might be able to pay the rent on a small factory loft."

Overjoyed with each other's ideas for the future, they raced to the elevated train and enjoyed the lights as the train sped over the East River and deposited them in Brownsville. Suddenly the laughter stopped. Jack grew grim.

"What's the matter, Jack?"

"Nothing. I was just thinking."

"About what?"

"About what to do with Mama."

Rubin promised not to tell the union leader's wife, whom he knew from Europe, about her husband's affair with Daisy.

Two weeks later, Joe Cohen handed Eslatka a union card and congratulated her on becoming a member of the Ladies Garment Workers, Local 65. That same afternoon, she got a job in a union shop that made high-priced evening gowns for special occasions. Her salary rose from eight dollars to sixteen dollars per week.

Eslatka was so grateful to Rubin that she let him kiss and fondle her on the bench alongside the woodstove. Rubin had fallen in love.

Jack's relationship with Bela progressed even faster. One night he didn't come back to Brook Avenue until the wee hours of the morning. Rubin was still awake.

"Jacov—Jack, I mean."

They both laughed.

"I want to get married."

"So do I."

"How do we go about starting a business, or was that just a dream?"

"And Mama?"

"Let's meet Louis and Nathan for dinner at a restaurant one night this week. They're successful business people. It's time we had a long talk and asked for their advice."

"Maybe they'll lend us some money."

That Thursday night, the brothers met for dinner at a local delicatessen. After they devoured the overstuffed hot pastrami sandwiches—delicacies they had never seen in Brest—the other brothers asked casual questions about Eslatka and Bela.

Finally, Jack grew angry. "Okay, already. No more small talk. Rubin and I, with Bela and Eslatka, want to start a dress business. But first we want to get married. Can you help us?"

"Hold it, brothers. One thing at a time. Do you know how to start a business?" asked Nathan.

"You rent a loft, buy some used sewing machines and a cutting table, and make some samples. The girls can design and sew, I can be the production and shipping manager, and Jack will go on the road and sell."

"I'd sell to the local stores too," Jack added.

"You make it sound so easy, Jack. Where will you get the money for the needles and thread, the fabrics, the machinery … and still have money to get married and eat? You think it's so easy? Ask us. There were times we went hungry and Esther cried. You've only been here a short time. Be patient."

"You bastards. You've got it all and you won't help us."

"Hell, hold your temper, Jack. We didn't say that. First, let's meet the girls and see about getting married. Maybe you'll be a little calmer if you get it on a regular basis."

Jack flung himself at Nathan, but Louis and Rubin pulled them apart.

"Stop it, you idiots," Louis ordered. "All right. If we like the girls, we'll help you get married and find apartments."

"But what about Mama?" Rubin repeated.

"We'll get her a small apartment, maybe one with enough room to get a boarder. For the time being, Louis and I will pay two-thirds of the rent. You two will share the other third—that is, until you make millions in the business you haven't started yet. Then we'll share Mama's expenses equally."

Rubin had to pull Jack and Nathan apart again. He grabbed Jack and headed for the restaurant door.

"All right, all right. Come back, you two. We'll call our accountant tomorrow. We'll ask him to recommend a professional business broker, one we can trust. I'm worried that some banks are not doing so well and have stopped giving loans to new businesses. Every greenhorn wants to start his own shop."

The younger brothers sat down at the table again.

Chapter 8

Soon everyone in the Sidowitz family was busy saving money for weddings and businesses. Rubin and Jack were working overtime at their respective shoe factories and turning out leather pocketbooks that Bela had designed in a rented loft on weekends. Eslatka, now known as Lota, had been promoted to chief sample maker at Gilda's Designer Dresses, Inc., and was earning twenty dollars per week. From her apartment on Brook Avenue, Mama Ida baked piroshkies and yeast cakes that she sold to the small independent grocers on every street corner in the neighborhood. The immigrant customers found them delicious reminders of home. Her business prospered.

On Sundays, it was a different story. Lota and Bela were planning a double wedding. It would cost less than two separate weddings and was kind of unique. They went looking for a hall that would accommodate their relatives and friends. Mama Ida made no attempt to help them pay for the affair but waited for the opportunity to take control of it.

Wedding dresses were costly; money was tight. The girls dreamed of lace and satin, fabrics they could not afford. Ida heard them whispering to each other and watched Bela sketching designs on newsprint.

"*Madlach*," she interfered. "Listen to me. Mrs. Blume in the next building rents wedding dresses. Some are a little faded, some worn more than once, but it's worth a look."

Tears filled Lota's eyes, but Bela said, "Okay, what have we got to lose? When do you want us to go over there?"

"What's wrong with right now?"

And they followed Ida out of the apartment.

"At least," Bela said, "we'll both have new wedding slippers. Rubin and Jack are making them now."

Lota smiled. "Rubin hasn't told me yet, but the other night he measured the length of my foot with a string. It was almost romantic. I guess he wants it to be a surprise. Though my English is not so good, I'm not so dumb."

"My boys didn't tell me," Ida commented sarcastically.

"The shoes are going to be made of white satin and decorated with glass beads. I designed them. Our future husbands—" Bela smiled at her future mother-in-law "—are making the shoes themselves, and the Italian women in the shop will sew on the beads by hand. Isn't that love, Ida?"

"I guess so," she snapped.

A sign across the windows of Mrs. Blume's flat read:

WEDDING GOWNS SOLD AND RENTED
Apt. 1A Ring bell softly. Morris sleeping.
No need to take a loan and go downtown.

Mrs. Blume greeted them with a "Mazel tov! A double-header, Ida tells me. Come in, come in."

There were racks and hooks everywhere. The walls and

doors were lined with wedding gowns of every size: stained ones, some yellowed by age, others with an occasional ripped train, and blue and gray ones for second marriages. Even Ida seemed disappointed.

"No new stock, Mrs. Blume?"

"Ida, don't be in such a hurry, Let the girls try some gowns on first."

"No, the merchandise looks too old."

"Come, let's go, Lota and Bela. There are other places in the neighborhood."

"Wait! Don't go! Two sisters, twins, dropped off a package today. I haven't even priced the gowns yet. They were worn only two weeks ago."

"And how many times before that?" snarled Ida.

"Never, I swear," replied Mrs. Blume.

Naturally polite, the girls turned back into the apartment. Ida stood at the doorway.

Mrs. Blume went to the back of the apartment and returned carrying two identical short wedding dresses. Each had a scooped neck and a fluted hem. Beautiful veiling flowed from arc-shaped headpieces and the sides of matching headbands that she carried in a hatbox. Each girl looked at the other and gasped with pleasure. The gowns were stylish, like the ones models wore in magazines and starlets wore in the movies.

"Don't be shy, girls. Try them on; it doesn't cost anything. I bet they'll fit."

Lota and Bela took the gowns and headpieces from Mrs. Blume and went into a small back bedroom that was used as a dressing room for her customers. When they came out, even Ida beamed.

"Perfect. They are beautiful. Now go and take them off carefully. I'll negotiate a price with Mrs. Blume."

Bela and Lota had no objections. They knew that Ida would get a good deal for them.

"Vell, for rental or sale, my friend?"

"Rental is good enough. I'll leave a deposit, a small one. The girls will pick them up and pay you the difference closer to the wedding date, sometime in June."

"Might be able to squeeze in a rental in between," chuckled Mrs. Blume.

"Remember, if they get wrinkled, you'll have to reduce the price."

"Isn't Mrs. Blume a piece of work?" said Bela. "And Mama is a pretty tough customer."

"Who cares?" Lota sang out. "We're getting married."

It was a beautiful Sunday morning in June, 1927. The girls decorated the meeting hall with seasonal day-old summer flowers purchased from the vendor who had brought them uptown from the wholesale flower district. He generally sold bouquets at the exits of the subway stations, but not today.

"I'm so happy, Bela. Are you?"

"Yes, but keep filling the vases faster. We need time to get dressed. I can't wait to put on my beautiful wedding dress. And I want to make you up so you look glamorous."

Lota did not quibble with her future sister-in-law but continued filling the glass jars, which Lota had painted white and highlighted with sparkling silver stars and flowers. Red roses were interspersed between pink and yellow lilies. Sprigs of baby's breath added daintiness to the homemade floral arrangements.

Mama Ida had mustered up a little forgiveness in her soul and cut out round floral tablecloths out of rolls of oilcloth to cover the dented poker tables that were reserved for Thursday-night card games.

She and her neighbors had cooked and baked the whole week before. It was summer and the windows were open; the weather was warm, and the whole street smelled like a delicious restaurant. Jimmy, the iceman, helped them deliver the turkeys, briskets, and chopped liver to the large ice boxes behind the hall that were usually used to store sodas. Defying Prohibition, the future grooms purchased schnapps and wine from a bootlegger and kept the bottles under lock and key in the apartment.

Bela had designed a *chupah* and painted the Lion of Judah on each of the four poles that held it up. Lota had stretched a giant tallith and trimmed the poles with pink and fuchsia ribbons. Rubin and Jack had rented tuxedoes, and the flower man had donated carnations for their lapels.

Tante Esther, legs spread apart as usual, practiced "The Wedding March" on the broken-down piano in McGullicutty's Irish Bar that was connected by French doors to the hall. Tom McGullicutty had always had a crush on her, so he let her use the instrument whenever she wanted to.

All the neighbors who had not been invited were hanging out on their fire escapes or watching out of their windows, waiting for the wedding party to leave their Brook Avenue apartment and walk across the street. The hall was attached to the tavern, the weekend playground for the local blue collar and factory workers. But this Sunday was special.

At six thirty the guests were already seated. Discreetly, the rabbi had entered the hall from a back door and was standing at a makeshift dais made out of two attached beer barrels, covered with the leftover oilcloth, courtesy of Tom McGullicutty's truck drivers. Esther started to play the piano. Ida, acting as the matron of honor, walked down the aisle regally attired in a velvet dress although it was summer. Since the brides had no intimate family members, the couples were escorted down the aisle by Nathan and Louis, the grooms' older brothers, also wearing tuxedos.

Ida was very proud of her four sons.

The primarily immigrant guests began to cry, remembering their mothers and fathers, sisters and brothers, boyfriends and girlfriends left behind in the Old World. The rabbi kept the ceremony short and sweet. When each couple promised to love and cherish each other in good fortune or in adversity, the rabbi pronounced each pair man and wife. The grooms put identical thin platinum rings on Bela's and Lota's fingers. Jack and Rubin stomped on the glasses wrapped in white linen napkins and broke them immediately. They kissed their brides with a passion that transformed their relatives and friends into a cheering crowd.

The Irish bartender came out from the bar, picked up Esther, and kissed her. "Put your legs together, honey; it's not our wedding. You're Louis's wife. Start the music, and let's dance."

Cries of "Mazel tov!" were heard all over the hall.

Everyone kissed and congratulated the grooms and their brides. The girls smiled and blushed, especially Bela. She was already pregnant.

Part 2

Chapter 9

By 1928, all of the Sidowitz family had moved to Brooklyn—not to the tenements of Brownsville or the cold-water flats of Williamsburg but to small two-bedroom apartments in the multifamily buildings that punctuated the tree-lined streets of Bensonhurst. The four brothers rented a two-room apartment for Mama with a combination living room/dining room/kitchen, a forerunner of the great room. Mama found a Chinese screen in a used furniture store and with it sectioned off a corner of the large space for a bedroom. To make ends meet, she rented out the bedroom to the local mailman; they shared the bathroom.

"Look at us!" she bragged to the neighbors. "For a bunch of greenhorns, we're doing pretty good. What a country!"

This was a step up the social ladder for all of them, but Lota remained in despair. She cried when she found out that Bela was pregnant, convinced that she was infertile. Rubin, no matter how he tried, could not console her, and Mama Ida sneered at her, muttering, "I had four sons, one after the other. Must be what the peasants fed you in Poland."

A few months later, Lota conceived, and her tears stopped.

Bela gave birth to a son seven months after the wedding. He weighed eight pounds.

Mama sat at her bedside counting on her fingers. "Aha, of course, you rushed Jacov into marrying you. So, honey, to make up for it, you'll name the baby Velvel—William in English, the rabbi tells me. That was my dead husband and Jacov's father's name."

It didn't matter to Bela and Jack, so they named their son William Kenneth Sidowitz.

Later that year Lota also gave birth to a boy.

"*Nu*, you'll name the boy William too," Mama commanded. But Lota rebeled.

"No. Your dead husband already has namesakes. In fact, three of your grandsons are named after him. Even your one granddaughter is named Wilma. *Genug.*"

"The more the better," Ida screamed. "All of your firstborn sons must be called Velvel. It's this family's claim to eternity."

"No," Lota retorted. "We will call him Hershel, Harold in English, after my late father who has no other grandchildren named after him. If you interfere, I'll take the baby and move away to my uncle. He has a basement apartment for me in his house in Canarsie. You can't rule our family. That's why none of us wanted to live with you."

Ida paled and remained speechless. She had not expected so much spunk from this daughter-in-law.

Rubin, always the peacemaker, interjected. "Why don't we name him Harold William? Okay, Lota? Okay, Mama?"

Unwillingly the women agreed to compromise.

Bela continued reading all the latest women's fashion magazines. Little William was a good baby, so she took him with her to Herald Square, where she studied current fashion and garment patterns in Macy's and Gimbels. She even took a sewing class. Bela sketched original designs, and Lota, who had brought a Singer sewing machine to her marriage, draped and stitched together beautiful garments at home while Harold William napped.

Jack and Rubin became known as the best sample makers in the shoe industry and worked for the leading manufacturers. After five o'clock they hurried to the improvised loft, where they pursued their own dreams of becoming businessmen. No more bosses!

One Shabbat they all assembled at Esther and Louis's house to celebrate the purchase of a two-family brick house on a tree-lined Bensonhurst block. The couple lived on the first floor and rented out the upstairs to a tenant. After the blessings, the meal started with chopped liver and chicken soup with *knadlach*, known in America as dumplings. Then they digested and rested a bit until Esther carried in the roast turkey on a doily-decorated silver platter. Bela helped her by carrying out a noodle *kugel* dotted with raisins.

"What a beautiful bird!" admired Lota.

"Of course it's beautiful," Mama responded. "Moisha in the live-chicken market always gives me the best. I think he has a crush on me. Is that how you say it in English? I picked that bird out for Esther's first formal Shabbat dinner in her new house."

Everybody laughed.

When everyone seemed full, Louis handed out cigars, and the brothers leaned back in their chairs to smoke and relax. Tea and cookies were served.

Esther started a conversation. "Lota, Bela, I was wondering. Don't you want more children?"

"Mind your business," reprimanded her husband Louis.

Jack blushed and interceded before either woman could

answer. "First we have to concentrate on our business. This is not Europe. America is a wonderful country, but we need more money before we can plan on having larger families. That's why we're starting a business. We want to become entrepreneurs like Nathan and Louis and own cars and houses."

Rubin, the quiet one, added, "Don't worry, Esther. We're just waiting awhile. When we're ready, our wives will have more children."

"Well, I think the girls shouldn't wait until they get too old," Mama said.

"Let's change the subject," snapped Jack.

The couples were not happy. Business was not so hot. Their new dress business floundered. The retailers and buyers liked Bela's designs, but women were not buying new clothes. They seemed worried about the economy and were saving their dollars in case hard times were coming. Even buying a house would have to wait.

Jack's smooth sales pitches didn't persuade the small shopkeepers he had usually convinced. He grew depressed. But Bela kept looking for trends in fashion. One day after a trip to Macy's, she came home all excited.

"Jack, I've got it! Money seems to be getting tight. I overheard women talking about wearing the clothes they had and giving them a new look by adding accessories like belts to change the look of last year's dresses. They're shortening their flapper garments and encircling their hips as well as their waists with belts. But there aren't many to choose from. I could design beauties, some scalloped, others concave, some straight. The buckles will be shiny metal, some with emblems. You and Rubin know leather. What do the shoe manufacturers do with their scraps? We'll need special needles for the sewing machines, but otherwise sewing is sewing."

She glanced at her watch. "Let's go share our ideas with Rubin and Lota. It's still early."

"You're wild, my *shayne maidel*—my pretty girl!"

They tucked William Kenneth in his carriage, and the family walked the three blocks to Rubin and Lola's one-bedroom apartment. After just a knock on the door, they walked into the house. In the kitchen, Lota was slicing up some watermelon for dessert.

"Sit, sit, there's enough for everyone. We'll just cut the pieces smaller."

After taking only a few bites, Bela could not contain her excitement. She poured out her dream about going into the belt business.

"I'll design the belts. Rubin, you'll go out and buy up remnants of alligator and lizard skin and leather from the shoe manufacturers. Lota, you'll scavenge the secondhand clothing stores and buy up cheap, frayed articles with interesting buckles. In time we'll find a supplier. Then I'll design some with the trademark Belabelts embossed on them. Maybe, maybe dresses will come later.

"And Jack, my handsome husband, go charm that blonde boutique owner on Kings Highway, but don't touch her. The street's a trendsetter, and she's always had a crush on you. Convince her to buy the first dozen sample belts that we make. Tell her that if she can't sell them, we'll take them back. I'll dress her shop windows for free and feature the belts, giving a new look to the clothes she sells. What's she got to lose?"

That night, the Belabelt and Accessory Company was born. The two couples celebrated with sweet wine as their firstborn sons slept next to each other on Lota and Rubin's double bed.

Chapter 10

ne day, Mama Ida dashed into Lota's house shaking a copy of the *Daily Forward*, without even ringing the bell.

"I'm here to play with my grandson, Harold William, but I'm so upset. Look at this headline, Lota."

Lota read in Yiddish: "Ford and other auto makers closing factories in Detroit!"

"*Oy vey*," she gasped. "It's terrible for business. Nathan and Louis will not get new customers at the station. Come into the kitchen. I have something cooking on the stove."

"Lota," Ida said as she picked up Harold and followed her into the kitchen, her inquisitive, dark, piercing eyes examining every corner of the room. "My regular customers have stopped buying my yeast cakes and piroshkies. Even on Erev Shabbat, they're buying cheap sponge cake and day-old bread in Feldman's Bakery."

"Oh? What has that got to do with buying cars?"

"Some are customers I've extended credit to who still owe me money. They even look away when they see me on the street."

"Can you think of why they have become so unfriendly and stopped buying cakes from you?"

"I don't know, except that money seems to be drying up. I've heard that a few of my neighbors' husbands lost their jobs.

A few weeks later, to his surprise and distress, Jack and a few other operators were laid off at the Wallace Shoe Factory.

"Boys, sorry I have to do this," the boss announced one afternoon at four o'clock. "It has nothing to do with your skills. You're good workers, but business is bad. The ladies have stopped buying shoes. So pack your tools and go home. I'll call you back if I need you." And Mr. Miles walked off the factory floor into his private office before anyone could even ask a question.

"Fuck him!" yelled Jack. "I'm good, very good. I'll find another job."

The men collected their personal belongings, and before they left, they kicked every machine in the shop. Hymie flung an empty bottle of soda against a wall, and it shattered into pieces all over the floor. Then they stormed out the door.

Two weeks later, at the exclusive Dell Shoe Salon, President Hoover's wife bought six pairs of pumps, each in a different color. Rubin had personally sewn them. Sam, whose work station was next to his, took a bottle of schnapps out of a sewing machine drawer, and the operators sat around celebrating that their jobs were secure. The next day Rubin's hours were cut.

The couples had been so busy trying to rise out of the lower classes that they had failed to notice the going-out-of-business signs appearing on many commercial streets. Something unkind was happening in the golden land of opportunity.

Jack could not find another job and grew increasingly depressed. Bela encouraged him to concentrate on Belabelts. Times would change, and then they would be ready to launch their company.

Ida had been the first to sense that times were getting harder for her youngest offspring and their families. She invited them over for Sunday breakfast. That morning there was no lox or sturgeon on the table. The all sat around eating bagels and cream cheese, drinking coffee and trying to be nonchalant as they talked about small things.

"Has Willie begun to crawl yet?" asked Lota.

"No, he still likes to be carried around on Jack's shoulders."

Rubin shifted the conversation from the babies to his brothers. "What do you hear from Louis and Nathan, Mama?"

"They're holding on to their business, but it's not terrific. The tenants in the small building they bought near the station are not paying their rent. One family skipped out in the middle of the night last week. Some people have little money for gas and are buying used tires when theirs wear out."

"Oh, my goodness," said Bela. "They have big children to support, and Louis has a mortgage to pay."

"Okay, *kinder*, let's not mope about things you can't fix. Sometimes life is good; other times not so good. Anyway, it's time to make a plan. We'll have to help each other."

"I must say that I admire you, Mama. You're a strong woman, but so am I," Bela said.

Lota put her arm around Rubin's shoulders. "Don't worry, Ruby, We'll make a living. I'll take in dressmaking. I'll charge a little less than the local tailor does for alterations and they'll become my customers. We'll be all right."

"Are you sure you want to do this, *susskeit*?"

He had never called her "sweetness" before.

"Yes. I'm sure."

"Okay, tomorrow I'll go over to the printing shop and make up some cards to advertise your new business. They'll say: …

Lota Sidowitz
Custom Dressmaker
All Kinds of Alterations
(Women, Men, and Children)

"When I'm not working I'll pass out the cards and tell everyone around the neighborhood how good you are."

"And I'll bake and wrap my cakes in your houses if necessary, so I can help care for the children," Mama offered. "Maybe we'll even offer delivery service for parties."

"I'll do the shopping and help Mama with the children too," Bela said. "While the children are napping, I'll sketch new designs for the future. You'll see, business will get better, and we'll be ready."

"Are you sure, Bela, that you want to get your hands dirty?" But Mama was laughing this time, not snarling at her as she usually did.

"Yes, I'm sure."

The hard, determined lines on Mama's face softened. "What a great family I have. With a little luck and God's help, Yehuda, my eldest son, will soon come to America too. We'll be all right."

The recession became a depression as life entered the 1930s.

None of the boys were in school yet. They played on the swings and seesaws under the watchful eye of their grandmother in the park across the street from her apartment. As there had been a series of child kidnappings throughout New York, Bela kept a constant vigil over them as they climbed the monkey bars. Mama and her daughter-in-law had reached an uneasy truce to cope with the family's problems.

Luckily, Mama's boarder, a bachelor, worked for the government. His wages were not affected like the ranks of the unemployed, and he always paid his rent.

The two older brothers fired a mechanic and a gasoline attendant and worked at the station seven days a week, ten hours a day. There were many radiators to repair and tires to align, because most consumers did not have the money to buy new cars. Louis and Nathan hardly made ends meet, but they hung on to their business, and Louis managed to pay the mortgage on his two-family house.

There was no new jobs in the shoe industry. Jack got a part-time operator's job in a handbag factory and continued sewing belts in the loft that they could barely afford. Rubin continued working, although some of Dell's customers had lost all their wealth. Mrs. O'Neal, the wife of the biggest realtor in the Bronx, hadn't ordered a pair of shoes in months since her husband had jumped out of the Woolworth Building. Lota was busy all the time altering clothes so her neighbors' husbands would look presentable when looking for work and children could attend school wearing pants that reached down to their ankles instead of stopping below the knees. There were few requests for three-piece suits or fancy dresses.

The recession grew deeper until it became a depression.

On the worst week of all in the economic indicators, Mama Ida's boarder brought her a letter.

"Mrs. Sidowitz, I took the liberty of bringing you this letter. It arrived at the post office this morning as I was sorting the mail. I knew you'd been waiting for it a long time."

Ida's hands shook. "Who is it from, Mr. Lieberman?"

"I don't recognize the name of the sender, but from the stamps and the return address it seems to come from Russia. You'll save the stamps for me, won't you?"

"Of course I will," she said nonchalantly as he handed her the letter.

She could tell by the handwriting that it could only be

Yehuda, the only son from her first marriage, whose father had been killed by a drunken Cossack during a deadly pogrom. He was the one who had driven them to the seaport when they embarked for America. Her hands shaking, she sat down at the table and opened the envelope carefully so as not to damage even a corner of the coarse sheets inside. She gently caressed the pages and started to cry. "It must be from Yehuda, but I can't read Yiddish."

"But you go to shul every Saturday."

"I know the prayers by heart."

"I can't read Yiddish either," bemoaned the mailman.

Tears spilled down her face. The bachelor put his arms around her and held her trembling body to his. She had provided him with the kind of home he had never had, and it pained him to see her unhappy.

Mama put the letter into her purse. Tomorrow was Shabbat, and she would speak to the rabbi after the services. He would read the letter to her, and she would then tell her sons what their brother had written. That night she dreamed that Yehuda was coming to America with his family after her sons had obtained all the proper papers for him, his wife, and their young daughter. His son, his wife, and their baby boy were staying behind. There was not enough money for the whole family's passage.

Chapter 11

As soon as services ended at noon, Ida hurried up the stairs to the rabbi's study. She knocked on the door, not expecting an answer, as Rabbi Bronstine was greeting his worshippers and sharing a kiddush with them. But she would wait, gathering her memories, until the congregants had gone and he came upstairs to remove his clerical robes.

It didn't take very long for the rabbi to appear.

"Mrs. Sidowitz, is everything all right? Why are you sitting here alone? No wonder I did not see you at the kiddush."

"Rabbi, I finally received a letter from my son, Yehuda, who is still in Russia. It's written in Yiddish script and I can't read it."

"Is that all? Come, sit closer to the desk."

She took a chair closer to the desk and handed Rabbi Bronstine the letter. He wasted no time, put on his glasses and began.

My dearest mama, my dear Jacov and Reuven,

It's been many months since I wrote to you. It seems that you are having a good life in America despite the depression we read about in the newspaper.

Life in Brest gets more and more difficult. Not only are we poor, but the goyim have suddenly become more hostile to us. I have heard that the Cossacks are returning to this part of Russia. Some say the Poles are helping them. The rebbe, and he's a learned man, says that the Germans are eyeing this territory too. Who knows why? There are only poor Jews living here.

Our neighbors have stopped buying what little we have to sell, or using my skills as a roofer to repair the holes in their roofs after this year's terrible winter snows. Josef is trying to continue his education, but the Russian authorities keep throwing him out for various reasons I cannot understand or adding fees that I can't afford. He is very smart but he doesn't want to be a rebbi, but a chemist, whatever that is ... something like a doctor. Can you send some dollars for his schooling, and maybe I can bribe an official to admit him to the science academy? We would love to send you a picture of our whole family, but we cannot afford to go to the photographer right now.

We want to thank you for all you've done for us. We have all the papers you've sent us to make it possible to sail to America, and Sarah and I would love to come with Mosha, but how can we leave Josef behind? He was married recently to Ruchel, the furrier's daughter, and a baby is expected in a few months. Despite the Revolution, her father is rich, because the land-owning Ruskies like sable, and he is a good furrier. But he is a selfish old man and will not help his son-in-law (our son or his family) as he does not want his daughter to leave Brest. As for us, we come as a whole family or not at all. Right now the old trapper is considering taking a new wife, who is much younger than he is and will likely have more children.

I know you wanted us to work with you in America and earn more money, but we'll just have to wait until we can raise that extra money ourselves. I hope it does not take too long because a dark cloud seems to hang over the Jews here in Russia.

Meanwhile, don't cry, mamele. *No one is fighting on this side of the world yet.*

I love you.

Yehuda Vinkovsky
Your eldest and firstborn son

Ida and the rabbi did not speak. The rabbi handed her back the letter, and she clutched it to her breast and walked out the door. She dreaded having to share the news with her children.

The next few years were difficult ones. The men worked two jobs; the women worked too. Old ladies still sold apples on the street. The economy improved very slowly. Cottage industries proliferated while mothers nursed their babies. The world turned upside down, and America seemed not to notice.

Still Yehuda did not come.

The children always seemed to need new clothes and school

supplies. Very little mail came from abroad, each letter hinting at ominous things happening in Russia. The Germans and the Russians had signed a nonaggression pact that contained a provision to divide Poland between them.

Here in America, the Sidowitz family celebrated holidays at Mama's house, and prayed that life would improve. They continued to send money to Russia whenever possible.

Hershel Velvel, Harold William, Rubin and Lota's son, was the grandchild asking all the questions even when it wasn't Passover.

"Bubba, grandma, how does Mr. Postman take his bath if you keep the fish swimming in the bathtub?"

"Oy, *totele*, Mr. Carp and Mr. Whitefish are only here for a few days. Emil, the postman, takes them out of the tub and puts them in a basin. Then he takes his shower and puts the fish back in the tub. No one seems to mind using the same water as the fish. Sunday your papa will kill and clean them. I'll season them and grind them up, and your mama will help me make the mixture into nice gefilte fish pieces."

"Eek," the child screamed, and he ran out into the hallway. Everyone laughed; they knew he would be coming back.

One Monday, Harold came home with a note from Mrs. Lerner, his young first-grade teacher. It was Mrs. Lerner's first year of teaching. She had rounded curves and a small waist, and although he was young, Harold was mesmerized by her femininity. He had no idea why she had summoned his mother to school.

"What does she write?" Lota asked her son.

"I think she wants to see you, Mama," said Harold, translating the English into Yiddish. "But I haven't been a bad boy, I promise."

"I know, Hershele, I know." And she hugged her child.

The following morning Lota wore the dress she usually wore on Shabbat and paid special attention to her appearance. She accompanied Harold to school a few minutes before class started so they could be alone with Mrs. Lerner. The teacher was at her desk when Lota and Harold walked into her room. Lota looked around, mesmerized by the colorful posters on the walls, the charts of the alphabet for the children to copy, and the blocks, educational games, and ropes stacked in a corner of the classroom for playtime.

"Excuse me, Mrs. Lerner, this is my mother. She doesn't speak too much English."

"Please bring your desk up to the front of the room, Harold."

"Yes, Mrs. Lerner."

"Thanks, Harold. Won't you sit down, Mrs. Sidowitz? Harold, you can translate for us."

"Did he hit someone?" Lota blurted out.

"No, no, Mrs. Sidowitz, Harold is a lovely child, but he doesn't speak English in class. He sits next to Anthony and whispers what he thinks are secrets to him in Yiddish, but Anthony doesn't understand him."

"Why not?" said Lota.

Harold was surprised at how much English his mother understood.

"You see—his mother is Italian, and they speak Italian at home. His mother wants his seat changed so her son can practice English."

Lota laughed. "As long as he's not hitting him, Mrs. Lerner, don't change his seat. His papa and I will talk to him at home and tell him how important it is to speak English like you, like the schoolteacher; of course, not like us. You should know that when Harold comes home from school, his grandmother, watches him and his cousin, and I come—I mean go—to a class for *grinnas*—immigrants, I mean—from many countries. We use the room right across from your classroom."

And Lota pointed down the hall toward room 205. "Learning English is good for my business, and I'll try to speak more English at home."

Harold was stunned. "Why didn't you tell me, Mama?"

"I was going to, but first I wanted to win the red dictionary for the student of the month."

"Did you, Mama?"

"Yes, I did. I forgot to show it to you because I was getting ready for Shabbat. Papa was so proud of me."

Pretty Mrs. Lerner stood up and smiled. "I remember when I came to America with my parents. I was only a little girl. It was a pleasure meeting you, Mrs. Sidowitz. By the way, Harold, would you like to clean the erasers next week?"

Harold looked at his mother.

She nodded.

"Oh, yes, Mrs. Lerner. I would, I would."

Chapter 12

To make ends meet, Lota augmented Rubin's salary by working as a seamstress from home, and Bela designed fabric and accessories whenever she could find freelance work. Sometimes the companies went out of business before she could get paid. During the summer, Mama Ida started canning pickles and tomatoes that she sold from a table set up in front of her building.

But the children were happy. They had thrived at school, spent hours at the local library, and played in the Brooklyn parks and on its safe streets. They assimilated at a pace no adults could ever match.

There were few cars and lots of gutter games like punchball or stickball and red light/green light while their mothers and grandmas sat on the stoops knitting, sharing recipes, and reminiscing about the lands and the loved ones they had left behind. The sidewalks sported jump ropes and hop-scotch boards drawn with all kinds of colored chalk.

Few new immigrants were arriving in America because of the quota laws President Roosevelt had pushed Congress to enact to keep jobs for those who were already here.

Lota sat at her window and sewed. She had left no one

behind in Poland, but she worried nonetheless when she read the headlines in the *Daily Forward*, the Yiddish newspaper, the family's link to the Old World.

One Tuesday, Bela came running up the block, her hair blowing in the wind, with Willie trailing behind her. She left him playing stoop ball with Harold outside the building. Close in age, the cousins spent a lot of time together. She ran up the steps to Lota and Rubin's apartment, knocked, opened the unlocked door, dashed in, and hugged her sister-in-law before Lota knew what was happening.

"Lota, Lota, good news. Jack got a contract today!"

"Talk slower, Bela. I can't understand you."

"Jack received an order for a thousand belts."

"From who?"

"The US Government Procurement Office."

"Why? And how did they find Belabelts?"

"I don't know. Morty Chernin, the college graduate in the building in the Bronx where we used to live, got a civil service job and went to work in Washington. His mother told Ida that he was a procurement specialist for the government. Jack is sending him an alligator belt. Maybe the pencil pusher's pants are falling down?"

The women laughed.

"Can we fill such a big order?"

"Why not? They've included specs, sizes, and required materials, along with quantities for each. And your husband's out on the street or down at the union hall already, rounding up cutters and operators. He knows who's a good worker and who's not. The ones he's hired are so grateful. Oh, Lota, our husbands make such a good team. And the loft will be buzzing with the sound of scissors cutting and sewing machines stitching by tomorrow. How wonderful!"

Lota grew sullen and stopped smiling.

"What's the matter, my dear sister-in-law? Isn't this what we've all been hoping for?"

"Maybe our country needs more belts for a bigger army and more fighting men. More uniforms, of course. I don't like what I read about Europe."

"Oh, silly, let's enjoy life while we can."

Their cheerfulness did not last very long. Mama Ida stopped by, and this time she looked depressed as she waved a letter at them.

"Girls, I think there is bad news. Lota, you told me that your papa taught you how to read Yiddish as a little girl. Can you still?"

"I think so."

"So, here—try. I don't want to go to a stranger, even though he is my rabbi. You are family."

And Ida pushed the envelope into Lota's hands.

Bela tried to cheer Ida up. "Maybe it's good news," she said.

"Dear Mama," Lota read, *"I do not think that I will ever get to America. Life here is dismal. My grandchild, Joesef's oldest, died of malnutrition, yet my son's wife is pregnant with another child who will probably be sickly too as she does not get enough food or milk. An ugly Cossack tweaked my beard as I left shul Saturday morning, calling me a dirty yid."*

"Oy!" mama screamed.

Lota waited a moment and continued reading. *"I am only a poor roofer, but I have improved my ability to write by studying and reading every book I can get my hands on. Now I expect to be arrested any day for writing about democracy in the Litovsk newsletter. Anti-Semitism is emerging again on both sides of the river that separates Poland and Russia. The Ruskies hate us even though so many Jews live in this city and helped overthrow the czar and aided the Communists to gain power, expecting a utopia. What they got instead was persecution. They are sending the able-bodied men, even the Yeshiva boy students, to work making war weapons in Siberia, and those who have gone before my son is called up have not returned."*

Mama Ida howled. "I'm never going to see my firstborn again!" She pulled strands of hair out of her thick hair, which she had pulled back into a bun. Bela grasped her mother-in-law's hands and stroked them gently until they stopped trembling; Ida put them in her lap.

Lota choked back her tears but continued to read. *"Others are being conscripted into the Russian army. Some say that once in the army it can be years before you get out. I worry Josef will be soon. They don't care if you have babies to support. What a mistake we made not coming to America when we had the chance. I would have scrubbed toilets to earn the rubles necessary to send for the children ...*

"Why haven't you written? No money has arrived lately, or maybe it's being stolen by the self-appointed officials before it even reaches Brest. The city is drowning in corruption. Although we manage to live from day to day, no one seems to know what is actually happening here on the Bug River, although Poland is in more trouble than us. Love you all, Yehuda."

The Belabelt business continued to prosper. They moved the shop into the heart of Seventh Avenue. Government contracts continued to arrive. Bela organized the office, and Rubin expanded the shop.

Rumors that President Roosevelt was increasing the size of the armed forces and uniform manufacturers were hiring more employees circulated on the street. Louis had sold off one of the gas stations and gone into the shoulder-pad business. Every military dress jacket required shoulder pads, and Louis was becoming a rich man.

The children were doing well at school. Mama Ida was very proud of her grandsons. At her synagogue, Mama Ida became the chairlady for the committee collecting clothes and tools for newly arrived immigrants, especially those who had gotten out of Russia. None of them had ever heard of Yehuda from Brest, but she continued to ask.

Lota registered for an English and Civics adult education class. It met four afternoons a week in a room just across the hall from Harold's classroom. The children often giggled when they heard the foreigners mispronouncing English words, but Harold never laughed. He was proud of his mother. Instead of a bedtime story, he helped her study American history from the *Learning My Way to Citizenship* booklet that had been printed in 1937.

Schools were not air-conditioned, and on warm days all the doors and windows were left open to catch the breezes. One June afternoon, the young students heard a commotion in the classroom across from theirs. Harold took the big wooden pass from the hook atop the blackboard and pretended to go to the boys' room; instead he meandered over to his mother's classroom. He peeked in. To his amazement, a spelling bee was in progress. Guiseppe, the Italian shoemaker's son, and his mother were standing in front of the room. The teacher, Mrs. Foley, said, "The final word is *democracy*, the kind of government we have in this country. The rest of the class be still. Can you spell it, Lota?"

Slowly Lota spelled, "D-e-m-o-c-r-a-c-y."

"Now, Tony, it's your turn."

Tony hesitated and began, "D-e-m-o-c-r-a-s-y."

The silence evaporated. The adults roared and ran up to hug Lota.

"You won, you won! A life on your head—*a leben auf dein kopf*!" yelled Lota's friend.

Mrs. Foley handed Lota a parchment scroll tied with a big red, white, and blue ribbon. Lota was overwhelmed.

"Lota, give a kook—I mean a look." A woman nudged her and pointed to the door.

She saw Harold and ran to her son. "My darling! Look, I have won a copy of the Declaration of Independence for being the best speller of the month. The whole family can read together and improve our English."

Harold dropped the wooden pass and hugged and kissed his mother until Mrs. Foley had had enough. She hollered, "Order in the classroom!"

They all returned to their seats. Then Mrs. Foley picked up the pass, took the child by the hand, and walked him back across the hall.

Everybody clapped. Mrs. Foley smiled for a change.

Lota invited Mama Ida for dinner that evening. After tea and cookies, the family gathered around the dictionary resting in the middle of the kitchen table, looking up words and practicing their spelling. The scroll Lota had won that afternoon was tacked up on a bulletin board on a nearby wall. The red, white, and blue ribbon was attached to the corner of the scroll like an official seal. The radio was tuned to WEVD, and lively music added an aura of happiness to the room. Even Mama Ida was proud of her daughter-in-law.

Abruptly the music stopped. The radio buzzed.

"We interrupt this program to report that Germany has massed its troops along three borders of Poland. It appears that she is ready to invade that poorly prepared country. Will Russia be next?"

The deep-throated announcer said nothing more. The music returned.

Stunned, the Sidowitzes sat around the kitchen table, no longer paying attention to the big dictionary. The Russian city of Brest was connected to Poland at the point where the tributaries of the Bug River separated and flowed into both countries.

"It must be a mistake, like Orson Welles's invasion story," Rubin said. "Why didn't Yehuda warn us sooner about what was happening in Europe? Maybe we could have done something about getting his family out."

They didn't know what that rescue could have involved, but Mama Ida burst into tears.

Chapter 13

In early 1939, the immigrants who had arrived during the 1920s and early '30s were so busy making a living or going to school that only some realized that Europe was exploding with political intrigue, anti-Semitism, and land grabbing.

Most of the inhabitants of the Brooklyn neighborhood where the Sidowitzes lived had family members still living in other countries, especially in the Russian republics.

Mama Ida rang her neighbor's bell one afternoon. "Hannah, did you pick up your mail today?"

"Yeah, only bills and advertisements."

"No letter from Minsk?"

"No, I haven't heard from Schlomi in weeks. And you?"

"No, no letter from Yehuda." Both women began to weep.

"Come in for a cup of coffee, Ida. We'll cry together."

Communicating with parents and siblings overseas had become more difficult. As relatives moved from one republic to another, from one country to another, to escape military aggression or political unrest, mail was often returned as undeliverable. On that side of the Atlantic, it was getting harder to secure passage to America for loved ones because of the quota laws, even when there were affluent sponsors.

Mama was constantly thinking about Yehuda and his family, still in Brest. Her male admirer from the temple tried to cheer her up, console her, and entertain her by taking her to Second Avenue theaters and Yiddish concerts. She was miserable, even as she helped recent émigrés who had managed to get out of Belarus, a republic now being demeaned and exploited by the Soviet Union.

Months went by. There were no more letters. Any news about Belarus came from the *Daily Forward*, the newspaper that Rubin brought home in the evening. Sometimes when there was bad news, he'd leave the paper on the subway and arrive home without it to avoid upsetting the women.

"Sorry," he'd say. "I fell asleep before the Twenty-First Avenue station. I dropped the paper as I left the train."

"I know you work so hard, Ruby, but try to remember to bring the paper home tomorrow," Lota gently scolded him, "so that Mama doesn't feel that we are hiding something from her."

"Okay, Eslotka." Rubin smiled. He found Lota irresistible when she called him Ruby. Their love had grown sweeter with each passing year.

"Maybe Yehuda's looking for us," she'd say and without another word, Mama'd rush out the door and run to her own apartment, sobbing, hoping that her boarder, the mailman, would bring her a letter or find an item of hope to read to her from the *New York Daily News*. He had become her friend.

Once home, she'd invade her kitchen. As she greased the tin pans, the clanging distracted her from her thoughts. She'd measure out flour, sugar, oil, and then added the melted chocolate squares. She dropped spoonfuls of the batter on a cookie sheet and put it into the oven.

Mama would talk to herself, "My firstborn is such a smart man. He's the only one who graduated from the Yeshiva. I know that he'll find a way to save his family and come to America."

Some nights the cookies burned.

Lota collected the daily newspapers that Rubin brought home in the evenings and stacked them alongside her sewing machine. Mama liked to drop by in the late afternoon and watch the children while Lota altered clothes for her customers. Lota would take a break, brew a pot of tea, and read her the *Bintel Briefs*, folksy letters from immigrants in America coping with the hardships of life in their new country and asking for advice.

"Oy veh," Mama would exclaim as Lota read. Together they'd laugh or cry at the narratives. Finally they'd search the personal classified ads. One that brought tears to their eyes read, "Leah and Schmuel arrived Wednesday on the *Vescovia*. Looking for their sister Hannah who lives somewhere in Williamsburg, Brooklyn. Has three children. Maybe by now, four. Urgent. No money for even a cup of coffee. (Contact us at Box #DF12780, New York, New York.)"

The writer was neither from Brest nor Yehuda Vinkovsky, her eldest son.

To her surprise, Lota learned a great deal more about the world from the *Daily Forward* than she had expected. She became aware of Stalin's third Five-Year Plan. Now instead of consumer goods, the Russians were building armaments. Farms were being turned into collectives. Synagogues were vandalized and then burned. The secret police were terrorizing the people in the non-Russian republics, confiscating their papers and property and turning the men into forced laborers. The Great

Depression in America had given Stalin the ammunition to promote collective farms, atheism, and communism.

Then in August 1939, it was reported that the Russians and Germans had partitioned Poland, primarily on paper. Only one corridor was given to the Russians: the one that led through the city of Brest-Litovsk.

The tragedy in Russia was turning Mama into a bitter old lady, always worrying about her eldest son and his family. She would share the ominous news from their homeland with Rubin when he got home at night and with the others on Shabbat.

Chapter 14

The rumors about the war in Europe finally spread throughout the United States. Every newspaper speculated about whether the United States would be drawn into the conflict and whether America was adequately prepared to fight Germany. By the summer of 1940, Germany had occupied most of France; Congress passed the first peacetime draft in the United States. Every male between the ages of eighteen and forty-five had to register with their Selective Service Board.

Families all over the country worried about how they would survive if their head of household was drafted. Some men enlisted because jobs were scarce and they believed that the war, though inevitable, would be short.

On Pitkin Avenue in Brooklyn, outside the Shoeworkers Union, Socialists and Communists marched in protest over the compulsory draft. There was still no war. Rubin and Jack marched with them. Lota, Bela, and the children watched; the mothers worried, while the children enjoyed the parade and banners.

As war between Germany and Russia began, some lucky families were able to flee Belarus. Mama Ida stayed tuned to WEVD radio's special hourly announcements, hoping to hear that Yehuda Vinkovsky had somehow arrived in America and was looking for his family. Many others did the same. At the same time, she worried that her youngest sons here in America would be drafted.

The left-wing newspapers labeled President Roosevelt an isolationist; the right-wing newspapers call him a scaremonger. Neither political party wanted to enter the war.

Walking home from the subway one evening, Jack quipped, "Where do we go to register? I don't want to be shipped back to Russia."

"Don't make jokes, Jack. Let's stop at the Democratic Club. They'll tell us what to do, because they'll want us to vote in the next election."

"For a few dollars maybe they can get us out of this registration mess."

"Jack, helping us get our citizenship papers without missing a day's work is one thing, but not registering for a possible draft if war comes could land us all in jail."

"The whole thing is *narishkeit*—foolishness. America is safe."

"Maybe, but only if the war in Europe ends in six months."

On Sunday, December 7, 1941, approximately six months after Germany attacked Russia, Japan demolished the US fleet at Pearl Harbor without any kind of provocation, killing 2,400 servicemen and wounding 1,202. WEVD Radio interrupted its programming to make the announcement. Mama stopped ironing her curtains, grabbed her pocketbook, and ran out, heading down the block to Rubin's house.

She dashed into the apartment, tears running down her face. "Lota, Lota! Where is Rubin?"

"Playing poker with his brothers at Louis's house."

"Do they know?"

"Know vat?"

"The world's on fire. The Japanese are killing our soldiers and sailors in Hawaii. Where is Hawaii?"

Lota took Mama into her arms. "Oh, my God, let's turn on the radio."

Fifteen minutes later, Rubin came home. The Japanese ambassador to the United States had left for home. President Roosevelt was ready to address the country. The poker game had abruptly ended; each brother wanted to be with his family.

War with Japan was declared the next day. On December 11, Congress also declared war on Germany. World War II had started. The United States was fighting two enemies on opposite sides of the world. Massive levels of manpower were needed, and the term of compulsory service was extended through the duration of the war. Registration now included all men eighteen to sixty-five years of age; those between eighteen and forty-five were immediately eligible for active duty. Rubin had just turned thirty-nine; Jack was only thirty-seven.

For the next few days while they adjusted to the truth that America was at war, Mama walked around, weeping and wringing her hands all day. "Oy vey, oy vey. Why did we come to America? My sons will be taken away to the army and their children will be orphaned. Who knows when this war will ever end?"

"Stop carrying on so, Mama," Rubin interrupted as he looked lovingly at his wife and patted his Harold's head. "This war won't last long. The Americans saved us in WWI, and they will now."

Secretly, Rubin was not optimistic. He suspected that his brother and the other Jews in Brest were no safer whether the city was invaded by the Russians or the Germans. As for Pearl Harbor: he wasn't even sure where it was.

On the Friday following the attack on Pearl Harbor, Jack and Rubin stopped off at the local Democratic Club.

"Hi, Sammy, what's new?" Rubin inquired.

"Business is brisk. The army is our best customer. Either one of you thought about enlisting?"

"Who'll support our families?"

Sammy ignored his question.

"President Roosevelt wants thousands of new recruits. Hundreds of healthy guys like you from this borough will be drafted. You can't fight a war on two fronts with a ragtag army."

Jack looked worried. "For how long do you think we'll be in?"

"Don't know yet. It depends on how long it takes to defeat the Krauts and the Japs."

"So where do we register?"

"Around the corner, where Jimmy's Fruit Store used to be. The produce is gone. The sign above the double store reads 'US Army Draft Board. Register Here.' Tell Ezra Cohen from Selective Service that I sent you."

"This is serious," said Rubin. "What'll happen to our businesses? We're married men with families. And I don't hear so well in my left ear since that Cossack fired his pistol at my head when I was seven and missed. Thank God."

"Doesn't matter, Brisker boys. You're in the right age group, and Uncle Sam needs you."

Dejected, Rubin and Jack walked around the corner. There was the store, now an office, as Sammy had told them. They entered a plain room containing army-issue chairs and desks and with fluorescent lights and got in the line for the letter *S*. They spotted many familiar faces. Overworked clerks were trying to speed along the rows and rows of prospective draftees.

A pot-bellied guy with an unlit cigar dangling from his mouth and a name tag on his jacket walked by, shouting orders.

"Hey, are you Ezra Cohen?" called Jack. "Sammy the Democratic Club leader sent us. Can you help us?"

"Wait your turn, boys. Just wait your turn."

As they approached the front of the line, the brothers were separated. Rubin faced a red-faced Irishman who appeared to have been drinking.

"Hey, kike, where and when were you born?"

"In Russia. When? The day after Christmas."

"Hey, Jew boy, don't get funny with me, or you'll be drafted by tomorrow."

"I'm not trying to be funny. All the goyem—sorry, I mean Christians—were celebrating. Trees were lit with colorful lights, and Mama was hiding me in case the Russian hooligans went after newborn Jewish boy babies, Mr. Kelley."

"Okay, shut up already. Sign here," and he indicated a blue line on the bottom of an official-looking paper. "I'll make you thirty-eight years old, but bring in your passport and citizenship papers so I can check you out and classify you—if you know what that means."

Rubin saw that Jack had already completed his forms.

"Jack, did you have your passport?" he asked.

"Yeah. I thought we might have to prove something. I'm younger than you. I'm worried."

Rubin tried to remember where his passport was. Maybe

Lota would know. She kept the records: birth certificates, insurance policies, their marriage license, their bankbooks, and other important papers in a big red accordion envelop under the bed.

Chapter 15

A few days later, Rubin returned to his local draft board and timidly approached Mr. Kelley.

"Remember me? I have my Russian passport for you to see when I was born," and he handed the decaying document to the rough Irishman.

Mr. Kelley made a few notes on Rubin Sidowitz's records. "Okay, yid. We start pulling numbers from the lottery tomorrow, but you're too old for the first batch of draftees. Lucky son of a bitch. You really are thirty-nine. If things don't get worse, the cut-off age for active duty has just been changed to thirty-seven."

Rubin paled. "That's my brother Jack's age. His could be one of the first names to be pulled from the lottery."

"Don't rush it, Jew-boy. The high school heroes are dropping out of school and enlisting in droves. They're young and strong, and they're what the army wants, although most of them are opting for the navy or marines. The army is getting the leftovers."

Rubin rushed to catch the subway to get downtown to the factory. He bought two cups of coffee and a Danish from the street vendor in front of the building and went upstairs to the Belabelt loft. Jack was already busy on the phone, extolling the quality of the belts they manufactured to prospective customers—not the beautiful ones that his wife designed but functional ones to hold up a soldier's pants under any circumstances. Operators were sewing. The Singer machines were keeping up a steady hum.

"Jack, it looks like we've hit a winner. Can we keep up with all these orders from the government?"

"I think so. Talked to Kimmel, the landlord. He'll rent us the adjoining empty loft, and we'll hire a few more cutters and operators. We better get an accountant to help Bela with the books. Lots of paperwork before the government pays, but the money is always good.

"The army has recommended us to the marine and naval procurement sections. They are so pleased with our following their specifications that they also want us to produce or subcontract out the manufacture of denim and canvas belts for combat and training. It seems the leather belts are only for commissioned officers and dress uniforms."

"Where will we get the money to buy fabric and thousands of buckles?"

"Bela tells me that the accounts receivable—that means the monies due us—are substantial. Even though Uncle Sam sometimes takes ninety days to pay the provider in US dollars, what could be better? I'll take the books to the bank with me and talk to Mr. Goldberg, the manager, about a loan."

"A loan? What if the war ends tomorrow and we can't pay it back?"

"You're always the scared one. Take a chance. The government is a good creditor. This is our opportunity."

"And what if you or I get drafted? Who'll run the business?"

"You're too old as of yesterday, my brother. And me, I'll try to get classified as 2-B."

"What's 2-B?" asked Rubin.

"Didn't you read the notices at the draft board? Two-B means deferred due to an occupation in a war industry. Every soldier has to have a belt."

"And what if things change and the war gets more terrible. They'll up the age limit."

"Then you'll try to get classified 3-A, deferred because of hardship to dependents."

"That describes both of us."

"Let's wait and see, Rubin. Meanwhile, they haven't scheduled to pull names or numbers out of the lottery cage."

"To me it looks like a bingo bucket. I feel so old and unpatriotic."

"What's the matter with you, brother?"

"America—it's our country now, and it needs thousands of soldiers and sailors to win this war. I'm strong and healthy, yet I'm going to spend months, or years, making belts."

There was silence for a moment.

Then Rubin fingered some of the belts laying on the cutting table.

"Nice work. Want some of my prune Danish?"

The war raged on in Europe and North Africa and spread to Asia. Germany had already occupied France, Belgium, and the Netherlands; it crushed Poland and the adjacent regions along the Bug River that, through the centuries, had often been claimed by Russia. The siege of Leningrad was under way, and the Germans marched toward Moscow. Britain and its allies fought back in North Africa, but Germany continued deeper into Ukraine.

The Jews were deported from the Warsaw ghetto to concentration camps; the German siege of Stalingrad seemed to be succeeding.

Defying the odds, the United States Navy defeated Japan at the Battle of Midway, and as 1942 approached, the US Army joined Britain and Australia in the invasion of North Africa.

Back in America, it became obvious that ten million able-bodied men needed to be inducted into the armed services in order to route the Axis hordes on three continents. No one dreamed that more than four hundred thousand young men and women would never come home.

Business at Belabelt was booming. Brother Lou was becoming a rich man by manufacturing shoulder pads for military jackets. Nathan operated the gas stations and, despite rationing, made enough money to buy a house. Jack and Rubin's friends were leaving civilian life for induction into the armed forces. Their wives, mothers, and elderly fathers were keeping their businesses open or working in the defense plants that were springing up all over the country.

Still Jack heard nothing from the Selective Service Board.

Routinely, he checked his mailbox every evening when he returned home from a day of buying materials and bidding on procurement orders, contracts, and conferences. One night, the ominous envelope was there—an induction notice from the draft board advising him to report for a physical on Whitehall Street in three days. He didn't tell Bela.

At eight o'clock the next morning, Jack burst into his local draft board and rushed directly to Mr. Kelley.

"Hey, handsome, where the fuck are you going? There's a line."

Jack paid no attention to the burly guy in trucker's boots and a leather jacket.

"Kelley, look," he shouted and waved his notice in front of the draft board clerk's face.

"What's your problem, Jew-boy?"

"It came. I've got a wife, a son, an old mother, and a brother and his family starving or dead somewhere in Russia. I thought you'd help me get deferred after I gave you one of Bela's gorgeous belts with rhinestone studs for your wife."

"Too bad. I remember you and your brother registering at the same time. It's a pity he got away because of his age. But now we're scraping the bottom of the barrel. We need at least a hundred thousand more fighters to crush those Nazi bastards and yellow Nipponese."

"Who'll take care of my family?"

"They'll manage. When do you have to report?"

"In three days."

"So go home and fuck your wife for a couple of days. It may be a long time before you see her again. But don't cut off a testicle, or I'll call downtown and tell the doc to stitch it back on. Anyway, if we didn't need the manpower, they'd label all you yids 4-F."

Despondent, Jack walked to the subway, intent on going to the factory, but he turned around and went home. He entered on tiptoe. Bela was sorting some ornate brass buckles that she had bought at a going-out-of-business sale. They'd look smashing on the newly designed marine dress uniforms.

He thought she was so beautiful, so American. Willie was at school. He surrounded her back with his arms, caressed her breasts and kissed the top of her head.

For a moment she was startled. She turned to her husband and said, "Jack, I like this matinee, but have you nothing else to do today?"

"Who cares? I've been called up for my physical on Thursday."

"Why didn't you tell me?"

"I hoped the notice would go away when I went to see Mr. Kelley."

"Did you tell them that you had rheumatic fever as a child in Russia? Tell them your heart's never healed. How will we manage? I love you so much."

"Guess what? My *narisha* brother, foolish Rubin, would change places with me if he could. He says it's our duty as Americans to fight for our country."

"Doesn't he love Lota and Harold as much as you love us?"

"As much as I love you and Willie? I'm sure he does," and he continued caressing her body before he unbuttoned her blouse. "But he loves America more. What's wrong with me?"

"Nothing, my darling. You're just scared. I talk to the other young mothers in the park. All their young men are scared, but Yankees don't show it. They've never been in a battle or seen the enemy on their soil destroying their homes and raping their women. They have never witnessed a pogrom, like you have."

"I might be gone for a long time."

"Even if you pass the physical, that doesn't mean that you'll be called into service the next day. But make love to me today, now and tomorrow too, just in case."

"What if Mama drops in?"

"Jack, darling, wait for me in the bedroom. I'll call Mama and ask her to pick up Willie at school and keep him at her house for supper. She likes that. Is that all right with you?"

Bela didn't wait for an answer. She went to the newly installed telephone on an Oriental-style end table in the hallway and dialed Mama Ida's number. She didn't care if the Italian woman on the party line listened in.

Chapter 16

It was Erev Shabbat. Bela pinned a lace square on the top of her head, like her mother used to do, and said the blessing as she lit the candles. Rubin, Lota, and Harold were there. Jack blessed the boys, sang the kiddush, and drank from the sacred cup. Everyone, including the children, followed suit. Mama made a *motzi*—a blessing—over the challah, tore off a chuck from the braided loaf, and passed it around the table for everyone to taste.

Before dinner could be served, Jack pounded his fist on the table and stood up. The children grew still, as did the adults. Jack was not normally a speechmaker.

"My beloved Bela, Mama, Ruby, Lota, and our dearest children, your uncle is going into the army to fight the Germans."

"No!" screamed Mama "not my youngest."

"Will you have to wear a uniform?"

"Will you learn to shoot a gun?"

"Will they make you an officer?"

"Uncle Jack, will you get a chance to kill Hitler?"

"Papa, Papa, how long will you be gone?"

"I don't know. Maybe until the war is over."

The boys ran to Jack and clung to his trousers.

"Don't go away," Willie pleaded.

Jack lifted them up and kissed their tiny faces, all the time staring at his Bela.

Lota was speechless, but she tightened her grip around Rubin's waist. He pulled her close to him and hugged her passionately, without any shame, in front of the others.

Bela, tall and statuesque, moved closer to Jack and stood facing her husband.

"Jack, don't worry. Rubin and I will take care of the family and the business." Her voice cracked. "Just take care of yourself and come back to me safely. I'll be waiting. I love you so much. I've always loved you."

"I love you all," said Jack, "but I also love my country. America is my country. It is my duty to defend her."

"Don't worry, I'll watch the *kinder*. Everything will be all right when you come home," Mama vowed.

"Thank you," and the two daughter-in-laws hugged her for the first time."

Rubin and Lota took Harold William home. Willie stayed with Mama. Jack and Bela went to the movies. They saw a love story about an Italian nurse who cared for a wounded captain after the British army invaded the toe of Italy. Fierce fighting surrounded the hospital; like teenagers, Jack and Bela necked throughout the whole feature.

On the way home, they held hands and planned an agenda for the days Jack had left at home:

"Saturday, we'll take the children to the zoo. Okay?" Bela began."

"Fine. Sunday, Louis invited the whole family to a big dinner. Let's not call it a going-away party."

"Jack, honey, Monday, the children go to school. Let's make love all day."

"That suits me, sweetheart. I'll never get enough of you."

Morning came too soon for the family. Jack kissed everyone good-bye because he did not know if he would be coming home after his physical. Mama held him tight.

"Promise me, my Jacov, maybe you'll find Yehuda or his family somewhere in Europe. How far will you be from Russia?"

Jack disengaged himself from his mother and fled out the door.

He stopped for a buttered bagel at the corner grocery and ate it on the subway. At Whitehall Street, he walked to the processing center for his physical. He expected to go back to the factory when this routine was over. Orders were waiting to be completed and shipped. To his surprise, although it was early, there were already lines of men going in. Others were muttering as they came out.

"What a pain!"

"Just why I left Russia—wouldn't go into the army. And here I am."

Jack entered the conversation. "How healthy do we have to be to be inducted?"

"Can you breathe? Can you see and hear?"

"Who cares that I get heartburn after every meal."

"They can still teach you how to shoot a gun."

It was forty minutes before Jack entered the building. He was greeted at a desk and assigned to a red-headed nurse who led him to a private cubicle. There she already had his record from the draft board—education, age, criminal history, marital status, and medical complaints.

"Jack Sidowitz, let's weigh and measure you."

Then the questions began. Jack was in a stupor.

"Do you have any problems walking?"

"No."

"Do you have any trouble swallowing?

"No."

"I don't see any glasses. How is your vision?"

"Do you mean do I see all right? Yes."

Then, she whispered, "Can you hear me? Good luck. What did I say?"

"Yes. Good luck."

"Follow me now, Mr. Sidowitz."

And sheepishly, without asking where he was going, he followed her down the hall to a room where men stood in a row; she left him at the end of the line.

An overweight doctor came, in took a quick look at the motley crew, and hollered, "Okay, you look fit. Drop your pants and undershorts."

A few hesitated.

Again he shouted, "This is the army. Drop your pants now."

All of them did. The doctor went up the row examining their pride of manhood and when he finished, he hollered, "Pull up your pants. You're all formed pretty good. Your blood tests will determine whether you have syphilis or some other venereal disease. Let's hope you haven't been fuckin' with every slut you meet."

Obediently, the draftees pulled up their pants. A nurse wearing a tag identifying her as "Nancy Grey, RN, NYC Recruitment Center, US Army" led them into the long corridor that led to many examination rooms for different specialties.

His first stop was at the podiatrist's office. A guy who had probably never graduated looked him over and chuckled. "If you walked in here, soldier boy, you haven't got flat feet. Go to the next office."

Jack found himself going from office to office, being

examined for breathing disabilities, heart health, hearing, and every function in between. Finally, he donated a vial of his blood for further testing.

"Hey, Jack, remember me? I'm Jesse. We used to play cards Sunday nights in the room in back of the candy store?"

Jack turned to his right. "Sure, and we were both losers. Where do you think they're sending us?"

"I don't know. I'm not even sure where the Pacific ends once it leaves California."

Finally Jack and his newfound buddy Jesse handed in their records and their vials of blood to the stern-faced, plump nurse at the end of the corridor. With a red pencil, she wrote *Accepted* across their files.

Behind her, just before the exit, two uniformed army privates were seated at a long table.

"Give me your right hand," said the shorter one to Jack. He took his fingerprints, filed them away, and handed him a paper. Jack Sidowitz was now officially registered at 39 Whitehall Street.

The private did the same thing to Jesse.

Before they left, the taller one handed each man a paper. It read, *Prepare for swearing in five days from now back here in the swearing-in room. Enjoy the time you have left. After induction, a bus will be waiting to take you to Fort Monmouth, New Jersey.*

Jack read the notice over again; so did Jesse. And the two men silently walked to the subway station and took the train back to Brooklyn.

Chapter 17

Jack went off to Fort Monmouth and managed to get through basic training without failing any of the required tasks. He was intrigued by the young soldiers he met, the different lands they came from, the multitude of languages they spoke, and the need to make English the language of choice in order to communicate with each other as part of a successful army.

He called Bela whenever he could.

"Sweetheart, I miss you. How is our son? And the others?"

"Oh, Jack, I love you so. My bed is so empty."

"Save the space for me. Mine is very narrow, but I'd find room for you any time."

"No jokes. What are they training you for? It seems like you're always in class. I thought they were making you into an all-American muscular warrior. The women like that look."

"Maybe that too. You may like it. I must admit I look pretty trim. But how is the family; the business?"

"Busy. Rubin runs it well. Lota and I help him. Mama even cooperates, helping us with the children. Everyone's English is improving. We are all becoming Americans. It's sad that it takes a war to do it."

"Be patient, Bela darling. I think I'm getting a furlough very soon."

"Why? Are they shipping you overseas?"

"Don't know. Have to get off the phone now; others are waiting. Kiss our son for me. Bye, love."

The better his English became, the more he was tested. He was beginning to think that an invisible officer was listening to every word he spoke. The tests he was given also included long paragraphs in Russian that he was asked to rewrite in English. He could switch from English to German to Russian.

A week later Jack was promoted to Private First Class and given orders to report to the Language Laboratory School at Dartmouth College in New Hampshire. He had scored high on linguistic aptitude and had been recommended for special services. Never had he even dreamed of setting foot on a campus—and such a prestigious one, at that. His son, someday, maybe … This, he thought, could only happen in America.

It was midwinter. The Russians had just recaptured Stalingrad. The Germans were fleeing west to Hungary and then, it appeared, returning to their own country. The Americans, with the support of the free French, reclaimed Paris and were racing across France. But first they would link up with British forces to reach the Rhine River. Eventually they reached the western German border. By the end of the year, the Soviets liberated Poland, captured Budapest and Vienna, and continued into eastern Germany.

In April 1945, American, British, and Soviet soldiers met on the bridge over the Elbe River, in a town just southwest of

Berlin. Figuratively, the war in Europe was over. Four days later, Adolph Hitler committed suicide in his Berlin bunker, and the Allies occupied the city. Along the way they had liberated numbers of displaced persons' camps, mostly the killing fields of Jews.

At that time, Jack was overjoyed at the thought of seeing Bela, holding her, loving her, and hugging the rest of the family too. He still didn't believe he, an uneducated escapee from Russia, had been chosen to be an interpreter, probably in Europe. Bela was intuitive; was the US Army preparing to ship him overseas? Is that why he had been given this final furlough?

To mop up operations and administer Berlin and the rest of Germany, the powers would need all the bilingual soldiers they could get. Jack Sidowitz was one of them.

Chapter 18

Bela and Mama Ida were sitting at the long kitchen table that also served as Bela's work surface and cutting table. She was designing a new pattern for a marine officer's dress shirt, and Mama was rolling out dough she'd then form into *rugelach,* stuffed with nuts and raisins, that she'd bake in the morning.

"Mama, don't you hear someone running up the stairs?"

"Why would someone run if they could use the elevator?"

"It sounds like Jack's footsteps."

"Oy, Bela, don't be foolish. All men sound the same. Learn to be patient."

"I need to be hugged and kissed by him. It's been so long since we've held each other."

"*Narishe maidel*—silly girl," Mama muttered, as she piled triangles of dough, each separated from the others by wax paper. She then put them in the refrigerator.

The footsteps grew louder and came closer to the apartment. Suddenly someone was banging on the door. "Let me in!" a man shouted. "I only have twenty-four hours."

"Mama Ida, it's him. It's Jack! The love of my life is here."

Bela dropped her pencils. The sketch pad fell off the table.

She left it there, rushed to the door, and unbolted the multiple locks that did not make her feel secure without Jack.

Jack dropped his duffel bag as the door opened. He grabbed Bela and smothered her with hugs and kisses, caressing her body, while Mama Ida watched and smiled. She understood. Once, decades ago, on a different continent at a different time, her love had been a soldier.

At last, Jack released Bela and picked up his belongings and they entered the apartment.

"Would you like a glass of tea, Jacov?"

"No, Mama, but I love you too. Come, let me kiss you."

Mama walked over to her youngest. She clung to him as if he were a child, only this time he was a man.

Finally she released Jack.

"Where's Willie?" he asked Bela. "Where is our son?"

Before Bela could answer him, Mama interrupted, "*Er schlufft,* Jacov. Come with me. I'll take you to see him, but don't wake him up. You'll play tomorrow."

She turned to Bela. "Pick up your pencils and sketchpad, and then brush your hair. Make yourself beautiful. After we tuck Willie in, I'm going to bed. Jack will come to you soon."

"Bela, darling, do what Mama says. She's a bossy old lady but also a romantic. I'll be there in a few minutes. This may be the last time I see you before I get shipped out."

"Where are they sending you?"

"I don't know, but wherever it is, your love will have to last me a long time."

Without notice, PFC Jack Sidowitz and a dozen other soldiers from the Language Lab at Dartmouth College were flown down to Fort Benning, Georgia, where they were taught the basic techniques of how to use a parachute by jumping off different-sized towers while hooked to a long wire. The instructor yelled out the nuances of body positions over a loudspeaker. After five successful jumps out of the plane, a soldier was deemed qualified. At night they studied their language tapes and attended lectures about the geography and customs of strategic areas of Europe.

Jack made friends with another soldier, who had originally come to America from Hungary. They sat next to each other on the long bench for the final practice jump, their parachutes serving as seat cushions.

"Egor, are you scared?" Jack whispered to him.

"Yes, are you?"

"Will we ever get home again?"

"I hope so," Egor answered. "My wife is expecting our first baby."

When everyone was asleep, Jacob would retrieve his penlight, a pen, and some paper from his duffel and write love letters to Bela. He would mail a packet of them the next morning.

"Okay, men, your preparation is now complete," barked a sergeant one morning. "Pack up your bags; you fly out tonight."

No one dared asked to where.

With little fuss, the soldiers were flown to London's Heathrow Airport. They landed on a foggy night and were unceremoniously whisked into a bus that took them to the University of Oxford in about forty minutes. A few of the soldiers knew that Oxford was one of the greatest universities in the world, and they whispered among themselves, but Jack was not one of them. He didn't know much about universities, but he missed Bela and his family dreadfully. He had to keep reminding himself that he was an American now and obligated to serve in its armed forces.

The following morning, they gasped as they were marched out of the dormitory through arches of stone that were hundreds of years old into a massive hall. Almost none of the soldiers had ever seen such medieval magnificence. Alongside the majestic buildings, the River Thames flowed toward London. This morning there were no rowing sculls on it.

The hall was filled, row after row, to capacity with men: short ones, blond farm boys, and olive-complexioned Mediterranean siblings, all young and enthusiastic gung-ho patriots. Jack felt out of place and uncertain, but he knew that he was a good linguist, and he loved his new country.

As General Mark Melina stepped to the dais, stars shining on his shoulders and his campaign ribbons on his chest, you could hear a pin drop. He looked tough. No one wriggled in his seat or dared to cough or sneeze. All ears and eyes focused on the general and what he had to say.

"Men, welcome to Oxford. You have been chosen because you are the smartest and best. Wars are not only won with guns and tanks but by infiltrating the enemy's ranks and population, listening and communicating information back to us. For that we need your skills with language. The information we need comes from everywhere: civilians, restaurateurs, shopkeepers, and factory workers. Everything you hear might be important to us. You never know. You'll blend into the area of Europe where you are needed most. If it's behind the French lines, you will speak French; if it is Germany, you will act German, dress like a German, and speak German. Click your heels and salute Hitler if necessary."

Someone booed, and a burly MP removed the culprit.

"Russian soldiers are now east of Berlin. Should you reach them, you will befriend them, have a few shots of vodka, not scotch, and speak Russian. People trust people who speak their own language and drink the same liquor they do. That's what you have been trained for.

"There will still be three additional weeks of training before you are dropped behind enemy lines. There is an isolated field not far from here that belongs to the RAF, and we have been permitted by the British to use it. Any questions?"

A skinny six-foot guy who had just begun to shave raised his hand and was recognized by a sergeant in front of the hall. "General, excuse my ignorance, but how we are going to get to wherever we are going?"

"Why do you think we sent you to Fort Benning? That was just practice. Tomorrow, you will learn how to jump out of a plane in the dark. It is imperative that we get you behind the enemy lines."

The troops gasped.

The general continued. "You'll be broken up into units based on your assigned destinations. You will get to know everyone in your unit—what they'll be wearing, how they walk and talk, how they comb their hair. It is probable that you will meet some of your fellow soldiers on the other side of the Channel. You will be supplied with a hand-crank generator to communicate with one another and with headquarters here in England."

A frightened stage whisper rang through the hall. "I'm afraid!"

"Who said that?" snapped one of the sergeants.

No one answered.

The general gave the sergeant a forget-it kind of look, and the infringement was ignored.

"And by the way," he added, "don't write home about your whereabouts or this meeting. Your letters will be censored anyway."

"No mail to Bela?" Jack whispered.

"This is not a day camp," the sergeant growled. "Any mail you receive will be held in London until you return."

"If we return," Egor muttered to Jack.

"I promised Bela that I'd come home."

"Good luck!" bellowed the general. "We'll meet here again before you get your final orders."

Then he turned and left the room.

Part 3

Chapter 19

In the darkness of night, as the Allied Forces battled the counterattack by the German armies during the Battle of the Bulge in April 1945, an American plane flew beyond enemy lines, away from the intense fighting. It was not its mission to engage in warfare but to drop linguists into safe areas from which they could, with the help of resistance fighters, reach the Rhine River and then cross over into Berlin.

The French partisans had instructions to get Jack to Berlin and hide him with Allied sympathizers in anticipation of the Russians arriving from the east. The other parachutists would be diverted to various sites in France and Germany, especially to the fringes of the battle in the Ardennes, an area of lush growth and small mountains between Belgium and France. They were to mingle with the general population and collect data on each of the countries: information that would accelerate the American invasion. Miniature high-powered radios were hidden among their possessions. The plane would then return to England.

Jack Sidowitz, fluent in German and Russian and capable of fractured French, was one of those men.

The linguists-turned-parachutists sat on a bench alongside a side door on the copilot's side of the airplane.

"Hey, Jack, what's the difference between chopped meat and pea soup?"

"I don't know."

"Everyone can eat chopped meat, but not everyone can pea soup."

"Hey, what did the lawyer name his daughter?" someone yelled from the back of the line.

"Sue!" answered a chorus of voices.

"Hey, yid, how does Moses make his tea?"

"Hebrews it," Egor the Hungarian yelled out.

Jack didn't laugh. He was too tense.

A fifty-pound pack of sustenance gear was tied to each soldier's leg. During the flight, a crew officer had sewn a patch in free-French colors on Jack's sleeve. The men appeared to be praying.

Sergeant Forester, the jump master, stood at the side door, holding onto a large lever that he would use to open the door when he was ready to send the guys out of the airplane.

"Stand up, guys, and hook up," he ordered. The sergeant pulled the lever to the right, and the door opened. Two brothers from Philadelphia were the first out.

Jack froze.

"Move it, Sidowitz, or you'll never make corporal," Forester ordered. Reluctantly Jack approached the door. The joke-teller behind him pushed, and out he went into the inky darkness. At preset intervals the others followed.

The white silks opened like the umbrellas in *Singing in the Rain* as the men steered to their final destination. All Jack could hear as he floated toward earth was Mama Ida's plea: "Jacov, find your brother Yehuda. I cannot live without him. He's my firstborn and must be somewhere in Europe."

"Yes, Mama," he had promised. "I'll try."

Sergeant Forester watched Jack and the others drop and then crossed his heart and closed the exit door.

A band of partisans waiting behind a grove of low bushes that hid a small field where onions once grew and a quarter moon were the only witnesses to this airborne ballet.

As soon as the soldiers landed, the partisans separated most of the parachutists into groups and sought the soldier who had been earmarked for the journey to Berlin. When they finally got to Jack, they inspected his armband and asked him a few coded questions. Satisfied with his answers, they nodded in agreement, helped him fold up his parachute, and led him away.

"Au revoir," they called to the others. In a battered truck, they drove this special soldier into the woods adjoining the meadow.

A partisan with a scruffy red beard sat next to Jack as they rode into the woods.

"Speak French, soldier?" he stammered in English.

"*Un petit.* Where am I?"

"In the Ardennes, near the River Ems. Your airplane crossed the Rhine a while back."

"Where are you taking me?"

"To the Elbe River."

"And the Russians?"

"They've overrun Poland and are heading like a steamroller toward Berlin."

"Will the American Army get there at the same time?"

"Maybe. Berlin is still five hundred miles away. But we'll get you there. You may have to represent a whole country."

"Let's start over again. My name is Jack."

"Mine is Jacques. Here are some peasant clothes. Put them on over your uniform. We'll likely sleep in the woods tonight.

There are hunters in the forest, and there's no amour there for the free French. Some are Nazi sympathizers. As we get closer to the Elbe, you'll get back into your uniform so the Russians—should they already be there—understand you are American."

Jack did as he was told. He checked his belongings and turned on his radio. There were no new orders. He would just have to trust his new companions.

The dented green truck drove onto a bumpy dirt road amid clusters of budding young trees and small hills. The French part of the Ardennes was a small sliver of France that was recovering from the desecration heaped on it by the Germans as they fled from the Battle of the Bulge.

They stayed clear of the coastline that led to the North Sea and got as close to the Kiel Canal as they dared. Tomorrow they would reach the Elbe River, the last waterway before Berlin.

Jacques was curious. "What are you going to do in Berlin?"

"Listen, observe *mit* Berliners *sprechen*. If I catch a careless talker or a bit of info, I'll send the information back to the American troops so they can stay out of harm."

"I envy you," Jacques said as he stopped at the foot of a small hillside, which was covered with wild flowers peeking through the remnants of the winter snow. He got out of the truck and opened the opposite door for Jack.

"Get out, Jack. We'll spend the night here."

"Where?"

"Here, just follow me."

He led him to the side of the hill, where an invisible entrance had been cut into an slightly indented slope. One push from Jacques and it opened. A fire burned in the man-made cave. It was warm, and Jack smelled a stew cooking. Probably rabbit.

"Elena," Jacques called. "Where are you, my sister?"

"Coming, Jacques. Did you find the soldier?"

Without waiting for an answer, a tall, thin figure emerged from the rear of the cave wearing baggy trousers, a thick gray sweater, and a matching beret. It could have been a young man, but Jacques had called her Elena. Jack noticed that she wore light lipstick and had a high-pitched voice.

"We have a visitor. He's tired and hungry. Tomorrow we'll row him across the Elbe if the British engineering company has completed the temporary bridge. Otherwise the engineers will row him across in the inflated flotilla they are preparing for the invasion."

"The British?"

"They are taking a beating but are making it possible for the Americans to cross into Germany. You'll need some sleep, Jack."

They ate the rabbit stew slowly. Jack savored every bite. Army life had taught him to put aside his ancient dietary commitments for the good of his country. And he was hungry. Every morsel was delicious. Elena served some French wine. He didn't question where she got the bottle. After a few sips, his eyes began to close.

"Where shall he sleep, Elena?" her brother asked.

"With me—in the back of the cave."

Jacques asked no further question but went deeper into the cave and emerged with some blankets.

"Guard the door, my dear brother. I've needed a warm body since Gaston was killed."

Jack had heard and in a daze he answered, "But I'm married."

"How long has it been since you held your wife?"

"Nine months."

Jack was too tired to resist.

Chapter 20

To his surprise, Jack didn't feel guilty when he woke the next morning. The lovely French woman slept contently beside him, a sweet smile on her face. Here in the cave-like sanctuary, both had been deprived of human contact for several months and needed to feel alive. He still loved and longed for Bela, and he prayed he would return to her in one piece when this nightmare of a war was over.

In the quiet of what he assumed was sunrise, he could hear the soft sound of storm boats on the Elbe. He could not tell whether they were coming from the other side of the river to counterattack or going across the river, further into Germany.

Suddenly without even an "excuse me" or a shout, Jacques burst into their section of the cave.

"Get up, you two, and get over to my shortwave radio. You've got to hear the news from London."

Jack pulled on his pants, and Elena jumped up, wrapping the blanket around her. They followed Jacques to the radio hidden behind some crates he had confiscated from the small village café nearby.

"Allied forces crossed the Elbe during the night with minimum resistance. It seems like Germany is about to collapse.

The race is on. Will the Brits and Yanks reach Berlin before the Russians?"

"It's time for us to get out of here," Jack said. "Get your clothes on, Elena, and come with us."

"Sweet Jack, I'm a Frenchwoman. I need to get back to Paris. We're sitting on a small strip of German territory that adjoins France. Although the German army is gone, it is not safe for Jacques and me to remain here. But he will get you across the river tonight."

The threesome drove to the tiny village closest to the river. They heard lively conversations in French and German emanating from a tiny café that, except for a red door, was hardly distinguishable from the fishermen's huts. Germans and Frenchmen had lived, farmed, and fished on this strip of the Ardennes together for hundreds of years before Hitler decided to change the map of Europe.

Jacques circled the small row of dwellings in the shadow of the hills and discovered a shed with a few remaining storm boats in it.

"What luck!" exclaimed Jacques.

"How will you get a boat out of there?"

"They deflate. That's my job. You and Elena go into the café and chat with the natives. I have things to do."

Jacques circled the row of houses again and dropped the pair off close to the red door. They entered the café. Elena ordered two café au laits, and they sat down at a small table next to a pair of German officers who had obviously eluded the American troops. No one seemed to mind that they were there.

"Hans, don't worry. Our comrades fled without waiting for us."

"Ist das Kreig vorbei?"

Jack silently translated: Is the war over?

"*Weis nicht.* Don't know, but we escaped the Yanks. They're probably waiting on the other side of the river and will take us prisoners if we get across."

"Not so sure about that. They're in a race with the Russians for who gets to Berlin first."

"So maybe we should hide out here, remove our uniforms, and pretend to be Frenchmen?"

"Sprechen Sie Franzosisch?"

Jack translated that to, "Can you speak French?"

"*Ya.*"

On this small piece of innocuous land, they understood each other's language. Jack too had understood every word. The months at Dartmouth had paid off.

Elena whispered to him, "Now Jacques has done his part. He probably has the deflated boat in the truck. We'll take it back to the cave and check it out to be sure it is safe and be ready to cross the river after dark."

"Elena, are you crossing the Elbe with me?"

"No. Jacques will go with you and then return here. I'll wait for him. Au revoir, mon ami. Perhaps we shall meet again one day when the war is over."

In the predawn darkness, Jack kissed Elena on the cheek. Then he and Jacques drove down to the river. Jacques had inflated the storm boat earlier, and together they pushed it off the pickup truck. They added a dozen small bottles of water, a weatherproof container with detailed maps and routes inside Germany, and boxes of ammo. They carried their guns strapped to their bodies.

Wordlessly they pushed the boat into the shallow water from the banks of the Elbe and jumped into it. Tonight there was no wind unsettling the waters; the river was calm and manageable.

Each man grasped a set of oars on either side of the boat and rowed to a desirable depth away from the shore. They then let the boat drift and uncovered the small motor that had been secured under the bow, attaching it to the vessel. No other boat was in sight, and the subdued sound of the motor brought them no unwanted attention.

They reached the opposite shore and docked the boat on the sandy bank. To their dismay they saw a mass of emaciated skeletons walking or crawling along the bank. After a few feet, some dropped from exhaustion; a few drank from the river water, ignoring the pollution from the boats that had crossed the Elbe. Mothers with shaved heads held half-starved and dead children to their breasts. The stench of human filth permeated the air.

Jack could hardly breathe. He coughed to clear his lungs. Both men were speechless.

An old man crawled up to Jack, yanked on his trousers, and muttered, "Ich bin hungrig, sehr hungrig."

Jack recognized that he was saying, "I am hungry, very hungry." He broke off a piece of bread from yesterday's loaf that was in his knapsack, "Hier, alte. Ich habe kein mehr."

"Where are they coming from, Jacques?"

"I don't know. There were rumors in France about camps for undesirables. The French Jews, especially the young ones, were rounded up and shipped to labor camps. We heard that the old ones, mothers, and babies were left on the road to die."

The crowds of ragged, stunned survivors kept coming. Some stopped at the sides of the dead and removed anything of value from them, including crusts of stale bread.

Jacques continued. "Jews, gypsies, priests, and anti-Hitler groups … The Nazis forced them to work in ammunition factories until they dropped from exhaustion. Then, I heard, many were shipped to a crematorium in Poland. The women were often used as whores for the military. But remember, those were rumors. No one is sure what happened."

"Where did they all come from? I don't hear any French."

"From the east, I guess. But now I have to return to the other side of the Elbe. Help push me off the shore. You're a smart American. You have maps that will help you get to Berlin and join the American forces. There you will find out the truth."

"Maybe. Maybe I won't. I just want this fuckin' war to be over."

Jack walked to the water's edge with his French friend. They gently pushed the boat into the water. They hugged each other, but only Jacques got into the boat.

Chapter 21

ack wondered if his brother Yehuda or any of his family might have escaped the brutality he was beginning to learn about. Could there still be a warm, breathing Sidowitz among these wretched survivors? If so, how would he ever find one?

He hadn't seen Yehuda or any of his family for more than twenty years. If Yehuda were alive, he would be an elderly gentleman by now; his son had been newly married and his wife was pregnant when he, Rubin, and Mama had left for America. There were some letters and pictures during the good years, but then nothing.

Western Germany was far away from Russia, and Poland had its own labor camps. Yet if the Americans were opening the gates of this camp, maybe the British or the Russians were releasing other emaciated, tortured human beings all over the continent.

Is the war over? Jack gathered his few belongings and started walking south with the survivors. He took a small bottle of water out of his knapsack and started to drink from it. A teenager who could still stand erect and move quickly darted alongside him and grabbed the bottle out of his hand, swallowing what was left of the water in one gulp before he ran off.

"Stop!" Jack shouted in German, but the boy continued to run.

"Stop!" he shouted again in Russian. "I'm not a German or a Russian. I'm an American."

This time the boy came to a halt and turned in his direction. His eyes brightened for a moment, and then the sadness returned.

He responded in Russian, "My name is Vladimir. My family is dead."

Instinctively Jack put his arm around the boy's shoulders.

The boy pulled away, but Jack was persistent.

"Where do you come from, Vladimir?"

Vladimir grew agitated, and a rush of Russian sentences gushed from his twitching mouth. "Vinkovsky. We lived next door to Chagall before he fled to Paris."

"That is a village just north of Brest-Litovsk, where I was born and grew up. The Yeshiva on the outskirts of the city had many students from small villages like yours. Did you ever meet a young boy with the surname of Vinkovsky?"

"I think there was someone in my Chadah class with the name of Chaim Sidowitz or was it Vinkovsky? After the Russians and the Germans burned down the Jewish quarter of the city, he disappeared. I fled into the woods, but a German patrol with angry dogs caught up with our group of resistors and shot a few, but they rounded up the younger ones like me as slave laborers and shipped us to arms factories all over Eastern Europe.

"I met Chaim again in a labor camp in Poland, but I only nodded to him. We were both exhausted, but I heard him crying that night and started to sneak over to his bunk. A guard stopped me with the butt of his rifle and returned me to my bunk. He wouldn't let me comfort him. I lost sight of Chaim when the barbarians rounded us up like cattle and drove us with whips across Poland and into Germany. They were terrified about what the Russians would do when they discovered the death camps. Their armies were just a few kilometers away.

"With guns pointed at our backs, they marched us through the melting snow to Germany. It had been a frigid winter, and although it was April, the ground was cold as ice. Many of us had no shoes and suffered from frostbite. The Krauts didn't care. The older men, women, and little children had been left behind to die."

Jack choked back a sob. How lucky that they had left for America in 1923. His son was safe in his warm bed with his beautiful wife, Bela.

"Tell me more," Jack said.

"I don't want to. Who are you?" the boy asked.

"My name is Jacov. They call me Jack in America. *Bist du Yiddish?*"

"It's none of your business."

"Yes, it is. I am looking for my brother or any of his children who might still be alive. Maybe we can help each other. Maybe you'll find someone you love too."

"I am not hopeful. I watched them being shot. They are dead. But I will go with you."

"Once in Berlin, we will locate the American headquarters. Maybe the commanding officer can help us. He should have my orders and, hopefully, mail from home."

At that moment, they looked across the river. Masses of humanity from another camp were fleeing south in the same direction they were. They could not see if they were crawling, pushing, stumbling, or dropping by the roadside. They were pretty sure that they were the remnants of captives who had lived through the torture of labor camps or detention camps.

Some were headed east toward their old homes. They had no idea if the homes would or would not be there. Most survivors, however, were heading toward American lines, hoping to find salvation as fast as their feeble legs would carry them. None knew where they were going and what would happen to them.

Vladimir and the survivors of the camp were living proof of the atrocities that had taken place behind the now-opened gates. Only when he reached Berlin could Jack hope that the war in Europe had really come to an end.

He didn't hear too much Russian spoken by the emaciated skeletons walking beside them. A man whispered to another man in German, "Meine Kinder, meine Kinder sind tot." (My children, my children are dead.)

"Meine Frau, meine liebe Frau, Ich kann ihr nicht mehr gefunden." (My wife, my love, I can't find her anymore.)

"Haben sie ihr gebrennt?" (Have they burned her?)

"Ich weiss nicht." (I don't know.)

The few women just walked, staring into space and moaning occasionally.

A convoy of American jeeps, a large red, white, and blue flag unfurled on the lead vehicle, suddenly appeared, slowly pushing the mass of humanity back in the direction of the camp. A six-foot American sergeant, built like a pro football player, stood on the hood of the jeep expounding in German, "All of you, back to the camp. The American Air Force has destroyed Berlin. There is no room for you there. We'll feed and clothe you at the camp until we can register you and let you go home. Meanwhile you will be safe. Please do not make us drive through you."

The survivors grew still and then turned around and timidly marched back to the nightmarish bunks from where they had come.

Jack opened his duffle bag. He took out his own small American flag and waved it at the sergeant, who motioned him toward the jeep. An officer with a silver bar on his collar came forward. Jack shoved his credentials into Lieutenant Hardwick's hands.

Jack spoke fast. "I'm a US Army interpreter who speaks fluent Russian and German. I parachuted into France a few days ago. I need to get to headquarters for assignment. This young man has helped me, and I want to take him with me. Is it possible?"

Lieutenant Hardwick scanned Jack's papers. "I think so," he said. "Get in the jeep. I'll contact headquarters when we reenter the camp."

"I can't go back," screamed Vladimir and tried to break away from Jack's hold.

Jack reinforced his grip.

"They're dead. My family is dead. I don't know who killed them … The Germans or the Russians burned down my village. There's nothing there for me. I want to go to Palestine. I want to fight for a land that no one can take from us. Please get me to Italy."

Tears ran down his face. He used his dirty sleeve to wipe them away.

Jack held the boy close and spoke softly in Russian. "Be still, my son. First you must grow strong. I'll try to get permission to keep you with me, to guide me to other camps in order to find our families, both yours and mine."

Chapter 22

A young soldier drove their jeep carefully and avoided hitting the helpless survivors who walked in a slow stupor back to the camp. Jack and Vladimir watched a platoon wearing goggles and heavy leather gloves dismantle the barbed-wire fence around the camp. The prisoners also watched them at work. The younger ones fled helter-skelter through the open sections of the fence away from the convoy of jeeps, while the elderly and weak survivors shoved and shuffled one behind the other through the open gates.

"Where are they going?" Jack asked Vladimir.

"Home, if they can find it."

As the convoy of jeeps headed slowly toward the outside world, a new mob of corpse-like humanity came limping from the east toward the gate. They had been marched here from Poland by German officers who had since disappeared. Although a Red Cross truck had followed them to this safer camp, all its food had been consumed. The men, women, and children hung on to the moving jeeps and begged for sustenance.

The American soldiers emptied their pockets and threw chocolate bars to the crowd; the refugees fought among themselves to catch each bar.

Jack was in shock. Vladimir accepted the inevitable and showed no emotion. Then the boy looked up and saw a gang of emaciated men clad in rags on the tower.

"Look, Jacov, look up." The men had picked up a German officer, still in his uniform, and were throwing him off the tower balcony.

"Kill the fuckin' German," the men in the tower yelled in several languages at the half-crazed masses. And the released survivors below did just that. They left the Kraut's body laying there to be trampled as they fled.

One aggressive survivor took off the German's jacket, tore off the emblems, and covered his threadbare shirt. Another pulled off the trousers and slipped them on over his naked legs.

Vladimir smiled.

The jeep reached the gate. The stench of death, decaying bodies, and filth attacked them. Jack gagged and stifled an urge to throw up. Vladimir didn't seem to notice. Lieutenant Hartwick and his men held their noses while they entered the camp.

As the jeeps entered the camp, the forlorn souls walking around scattered to the side of the wide thoroughfare to avoid being run over. They did not seem to know that they had been liberated.

A street sign read Mittelstrasse. The road split the camp into two sections. There were no doors on the green concrete buildings that lined the long entrance to the camp. When the GIs looked inside the numerous buildings, they saw rows and rows of bunks stacked six high, reaching from the ground to the ceilings.

Jack poked Vladimir. "Which bunk did you sleep in?"

"Number six, most of the time. Sometimes I was summoned to the commandant's house. I was his plaything, his pet. If I was good, he'd reward me with a piece of roast beef or a piece of potato kugel. That's why I'm not as starved as the others."

"You let him molest you?"

"I did anything to stay alive. So did everyone else."

Jack was speechless.

Weary men, some in faded striped pajamas, most with a yellow Star of David pinned on them, lay prone on the bunk beds. There appeared to be no mattresses. The occasional movement from a hand or a leg reassured Jack, Vladimir, and the soldiers that some of the skeleton-like figures were still alive. They could see men wetting their lips with their tongues, as if saliva were their only source of fluid. Jack surmised that the forced laborers had not been bused to the munitions factories; nor had they been given anything to eat or drink that day. But no one had told them why, and they appeared listless and confused.

In buildings on the left side of the wide avenue, women and children were stretched out on the bare bunks as if they were already dead. Occasionally, a child had the strength to scream, and a mother's song could be heard trying to comfort him.

The jeeps continued up the drive until a huge pyre of logs blocked them from continuing to the commandant's headquarters that they would convert into the division office where they would hook up radios and communicate with headquarters. As the jeeps approached the pyre, Vladimir covered his eyes with his hands.

"Will the soldiers burn the bodies?"

"What bodies?"

And Jack looked again and saw at least two hundred naked men stacked atop the logs to be burned, but the Germans had run out of time. He blinked and realized that these men were already dead.

Vladimir's face paled, but he remained stoic. Jack held him close, and for the first time, Vladimir did not pull away. The pair, like a father and son, gave each other strength.

The convoy waited until a group of soldiers with picks and shovels was summoned to the front of the lead jeep; they removed the pyre. Then they dug a trench on the perimeter of the camp and buried the bodies.

"Next time," Lieutenant Hardwick exclaimed to his men, "we'll make the villagers bury their victims."

The survivors who could still stand in the narrow alleys between the concrete buildings saw and heard it all.

As the soldiers covered the open trench with blood-stained soil, Vladimir wept for the first time since he and Jack had met, his head held high while his body quivered.

Jack stood in the moving jeep and intoned the centuries-old Mourner's Kaddish. A few soldiers in some of the other jeeps noticed Jack, and they joined him and chanted the sacred prayer for the dead that many had learned years earlier from their fathers or in religious school. Suddenly all the soldiers rose in their jeeps and prayed for the souls of not only the Jews but the Catholics, gypsies, and the righteous gentiles who had been tortured and killed in inhuman ways by the Nazis. A group of survivors mustered their remaining strength and added their melancholy tones to the communal respect for the dead. The need for God to sustain life echoed throughout the camp. Vladimir was too angry to join them.

Then the jeeps continued up the wide road to the former commandant's dwelling.

Chapter 23

ack and Vladimir looked on in awe as the baby-faced recruits proceeded to set up a functioning unit in the commandant's house. Magically from somewhere in the convoy, a white sheet appeared, and on it a pimply faced private wielding a black marker printed:

Unit B5
Second Battalion
Thirty-Ninth Division
United States Army

Two other soldiers nailed it above the front door.

A group of army cooks started dragging out pots and pans, a portable stove, and cartons of food, most of which appeared to be canned. They set up an outdoor kitchen and started cooking. The scent caused the frail and hungry survivors to stumble out of their green buildings in search of anything to eat.

A staff sergeant assigned groups of men to various abandoned buildings, where they deposited their bedrolls and reappeared for assignment. MPs hurried to staff the gate so no one could come in or go out of the camp without written permission.

Lieutenant Hardwick came out of the house with a megaphone in one hand and stood on a crate of abandoned German books so everyone could see him. He waited for the whispering to stop.

"Good day, my friends. I am Lieutenant Hardwick. Guten Tag meine freunde. Ich bin Lieutenant Hardwick."

More survivors crept out of the green buildings to listen. Jack strode up beside him and translated the following words into Russian.

"We are American soldiers from the Second Battalion, Thirty-Ninth Division of the US Army. We are not here to hurt you but to protect and care for you now that you are liberated.

"No one will beat or torture you. The factories will be dismantled. You will no longer be forced to make armaments for the Krauts. But we cannot just release you because the Germans have not yet totally surrendered and the war is not officially over.

"In a few days, a unit from the Office of Military Government will arrive to register you and allow those who want to go home to leave. If you have nowhere to go, this camp will serve as a displaced persons facility until other arrangements can be made. It has been a long, hard war, and all of us want to go home."

Silence reigned as Jack also translated the lieutenant's every word into German. He realized now why he had been sent to Dartmouth.

"You are now free men and women, but we need your cooperation to get you healthy and keep you safe. Each morning I will speak with you and inform you of any changes or new rules we need to follow. Supper will be ready soon, and you will eat."

Once Jack had translated, he said to him, "I must call Berlin.

The radios have been set up. Corporal Sidowitz, take over." And he pinned two stripes on Jack's right sleeve.

Jack said, "Sir, they are expecting me in Berlin. Will you let them know that I am here? What are my orders? And are they holding any mail for me?"

"Yes, Corporal, I will, but I'm glad you're here, Frankly, I have a lot of questions myself. We need provisions and medicine, perhaps an extra doctor. This is one of the first camps to be liberated, and I'm running this operation by the seat of my pants. Look how sick they are. I have only one doctor, a green intern from Baltimore. He has never seen such misery. Neither have I. Perhaps there are survivors who were once nurses or midwives, or even a stray doctor who managed to hide his identity from the Krauts."

"Vladimir and I will try and find them for you."

"I hear that in all this depravity, a young woman is expecting to give birth any moment."

Jack could not resist. "Sir, there will be new life in this abysmal place after all. Vladimir, let's get some help for the mother-to-be, and maybe we'll find out if any from our destroyed cities survived. Are we dismissed, Lieutenant?"

"Dismissed."

That night, Mona Rosenzweig gave birth to a six-pound baby girl. No one, including Mona, knew who the father was. She had been raped by several camp guards, but she had stayed alive. She held her baby to her breast, swearing she would never tell her how she was conceived or where she was born. The baby was delivered by an ancient survivor in bunk seventeen who had been a midwife in the city of Minsk twenty years earlier.

Like riding a bicycle, Jack thought, *there are some things you never forget.*

The whole camp celebrated. A few soldiers collected refuse all over the camp for fuel and ignited a bonfire, the kind they had back home in the Kentucky hills. Several bottles of schnapps surfaced from nowhere and were passed around. A survivor started playing a harmonica that had been hidden for so long in his damp clothing that it sounded rusty. Three frail bunkmates rose from their beds and danced for a few moments before they collapsed back on their bunks with smiles on their faces. The soldiers clapped and stamped their feet to the rhythm of the music.

The baby nursed and then slept peacefully in her mother's arms.

The following morning, a military truck, loaded with supplies of food, clothing, bars of soap, clean blankets, and, miraculously, a dozen diapers, pulled into the camp. The soldier in the passenger seat opened his window and hollered loud and clear, "We've got stacks of mail, guys, but be patient."

They parked the truck in a clearing alongside the commander's headquarters.

Lieutenant Hardwick came out and welcomed the driver with open arms as a staff sergeant ordered the men to unpack the truck and organize the supplies for distribution. Checklists and receipts were exchanged.

Finally, a booming voice echoed through the camp. "Mail call. Come and get it, boys!" Every soldier not on guard duty or engaged in a priority assignment rushed to the clearing.

Jack was nervous. Had Bela written?

The staff sergeant was already calling out names and handing out mail. "Brown, Philip. Schmidt, Joseph. Johanson, Nils. Esposito, Pete. Sidowitz, Jack."

Jack ran to the front of the group and grabbed the package of letters tied together with rough cord out of the officer's hands before he could toss them to him. He recognized his wife's handwriting on the top envelope and kissed it lightly.

"Sergeant!" he shouted. "Can we mail letters back home? I've been writing to my wife every day, and I have a bundle of them for her to share with my mother and brothers."

"Sure, guys, just don't jump me. I have to deliver some important papers to Lieutenant Hardwick. I'll let you know before I'm ready to drive back to Berlin."

And he entered the unit's headquarters, as the soldiers started opening their mail.

Almost ten minutes later, a clerk came out of the headquarters and beckoned Jack to come inside with him. Jack assumed he had more translating to do. Lieutenant Hardwick was waiting for him.

"Have a seat, Corporal. Your orders have arrived with the mail. I hate to lose you, but that's war. General Traymore needs you in Berlin. The loudmouthed Russians are clogging the streets as they enter from the east. He wants to know what they're saying. Sergeant Drumm will drive you there."

"Can I bring Vladimir with me?"

"What the hell? Why not? The orders didn't say no, and I suspect you have a secret agenda."

Jack pretended not to hear the officer.

"When do we leave?" he asked.

"Tomorrow morning, right after mess. Meanwhile, get lost somewhere and read your mail. You're holding those letters so close to you, you'd think your woman was real."

"Oh, how I wish she were. Thanks for everything, Lieutenant."

And Jack strode over to the only grove of trees the Nazis had left standing in one corner of the barren, dusty camp.

Chapter 24

Darling Jack,

Every morning I wake up hungry for you. And I worry. We haven't heard from you in so long. Mama Ida is a wreck. They tell me that no news is good news, so I am glad that a local policeman hasn't brought a representative of the US Army to our door.

Every night as I put our son to bed, I pretend you are with me, standing behind me, holding me around the waist, so close that I can feel every muscle in your body pressing into mine. I can't wait for our angel to fall asleep so we can go to our bed and love each other in every way possible.

Belabelts is making lots of money because of this nasty war. Have no idea of what will happen when it ends, so I am saving as much as I can. The army and marines keep ordering more belts as more and more boys are drafted and many are sent on to officers training school. Have you been promoted yet?

Rubin and Lota are great factory managers, and I am busy designing and selling. We listen to the news on the radio constantly and try to figure out where you are and what you are doing as the fortunes of this war change.

Their children, like ours, are growing rapidly and learning about war prematurely. Mrs. Kornfeld's son Heshie just came home minus a leg, and they see him hobbling on his crutches to the bus stop on the corner every day when he goes to the VA hospital for physical therapy. He doesn't smile too much.

The boys ask questions, and I try to explain, saying that your daddy, and Harold's uncle, is okay. He's a great hero and so valuable that the army is looking after him. At this age, they believe everything I tell them.

Jack held back his tears.

Mama Ida is the most depressed person here. She goes on and on about Yehuda and his family. The only hope that keeps her alive, I think, is that you will find him or one of his children. Is that a pipe dream? She doesn't realize that you might be in danger yourself. She has no idea how big Europe is or where he could be. No word ever comes from Brest. Don't they allow mail out of the country, or are the Germans occupying that part of Russia?

We are starting to hear some terrible things about what has happened in Europe. So many of our neighbors are missing relatives or have sons fighting in Europe. Others are in places most of us never heard of.

Please, please, God, let my love get this letter. It is stained with tears and kisses. May this horrible conflict end, and may He bring you home safely to us.

All my love, all my love,
Bela

Chapter 25

At six thirty the next morning, Jack and Vladimir were in the jeep with Sergeant Drumm heading toward Berlin. They hoped that they had left the furnaces and stacks of dead bodies behind them, but the displaced walking cadavers on the sides of the road silently said otherwise. They had no idea what to expect.

Two armed soldiers sat behind them. "Where are they all going?" asked one of the soldiers.

"Don't know," answered his partner.

"Where did you learn to speak so many languages, Corporal?" a soldier asked.

"I was an immigrant to America from Russia, so I spoke bad Russian and a little German. I was a salesman in New York City, so I had to learn English fast. By the time I was drafted, my English was pretty good. The army tested me and decided that I had a knack for languages. So they sent me to language school.

"I can't even speak Spanish, and my parents came from Puerto Rico. You must be a smart guy."

The closer they got to Berlin, the more devastated the land became. Instead of houses, windowless walls reached for nowhere. Mountains of rubble—bricks, broken bottles, fractured furniture, and baby carriages—filled former sidewalks and streets in outlying towns. Occasionally, a lone person came into sight and disappeared behind the rubble or into a lonesome doorway when they saw the vehicle with USA painted on the side. A damaged church steeple hung precariously toward earth, threatening to crash down on anyone who dared to walk beneath it.

The second soldier volunteered some information. "Those Russians really beat the crap out of them, and our bombers did the rest."

"They deserved to be annihilated!" Vladimir screamed. "They burned our fields of ripening grain so that we would starve. Then they raped our women as their children watched and burned our houses with the women and children in them. The Germans were animals and showed no mercy. May their cities burn in hell."

His tragic tone sobered up the two soldiers when Jack translated Vladimir's words into English.

The jeep entered Berlin in the early afternoon. People were walking everywhere, dragging carts filled with household items in all directions, as if no one was certain where they were going. Berlin had become a city of women. Russian soldiers shoved crippled German soldiers and women and children from the broken sidewalks into the middle of the rutted road.

A Russian soldier, his fists in the air, his head lifted to the sky, laughed as he yelled out, "Berlin is ours. You are ours. We will do with you what we will." Jack interpreted for the others.

They heard whispers about Hitler and Frau Eva Braun but could not make out the hushed conversations from the mass of homeless walkers. To the amazement of the onlookers, Sergeant

Drumm, sporting an American flag, stopped the jeep. Jack got out of the jeep and spoke to an elderly man in perfect German.

"Was hast beshert?" (What has happened?)

"Hitler ist tod! Wir haben das Krieg verlosen!" (Hitler is dead! We have lost the war!)

Returning to the jeep, Corporal Sidowitz shared the news with the others.

Vladimir erupted. "They should have burned the fuckin' lovers alive!"

Jack did not bother to translate the young Russian's exclamation to the American soldiers.

Though it seemed like the war in Germany was over, Jack Sidowitz's mission had just begun. He had a plan, but would his superiors allow him to search for his brother among the chaos on the Continent? He had promised his mother to do so.

Sergeant Drumm proceeded to the army's temporary headquarters at the Gershon Air Force building alongside Das Reichstag. An American flag flew above its arched entrance.

Sergeant Drumm escorted Jack and Vladimir into the American headquarters, up a flight of marble stairs. A row of offices overlooked an ornate hall that had been stripped of its paintings. A variety of squares and rectangles from frames that had once held art masterpieces were left behind.

On the door numbered 217, a new bronze plaque read "Col. Robert L. Soberman, Administrative Officer, USA." The sergeant knocked. Someone on the inside peered through a peephole.

"Seven four one seven seven six," the sergeant whispered. There was a click; the door was unlocked and the threesome approached.

The guard recognized Sergeant Drumm and let him pass.

"May I see your papers?" he asked the other two.

Jack produced his papers and handed them to the guard.

"You're okay, Corporal. But who's this skinny runt?"

"An ex-German prisoner. Found him leaving the camp, headed for Berlin, an example of the exodus to come now that the camps are liberated."

"Between the Russians, the leftover Krauts, and the half-naked refugees, Berlin is a fucked-up city!"

"Watch your mouth, soldier," the sergeant barked.

They entered the office, and Jack introduced himself. "Good day, Colonel Soberman. I'm Corporal Sidowitz, the interpreter you asked for, and this is my unofficial guide, Vladimir, now a displaced person."

"You look like the Lord of La Mancha and his steward, Sancho Panza! I loved Cervantes's book *Don Quixote*."

Corporal Sidowitz didn't crack a smile. The army had not sent him to Dartmouth to study Spanish literature. He had no idea who Cervantes was, and Vladimir certainly didn't.

"I'm sorry, Corporal. I wasn't trying to be funny. I know you weren't educated in the US. I'm a Jew too, and this assignment is giving me an ulcer. But who can do it better than us, who feel their misery and their pain? I've been expecting you. There'll be lots of meetings where I'll need you to interpret. Also a few translations … We need to understand the Russians and the Germans, and they need to understand us."

Then he pointed to Vladimir. "Why is he here?"

"He escaped from a camp in the east and got caught. Because of his youth and fitness, he was sent to Sachsenhausen, a labor camp. He walked out of the camp when the Americans liberated it. It was such chaos that nobody cared. He's attached himself to me. He's a survivor. His Russian and German are impeccable, and he knows his way around. He's helped me get my bearings and communicate with the unfortunates still in the camps with nowhere to go. Actually, Vladimir wants to get to the farthest camp in southern Europe—even if he has to walk there. At least he'll be closer to Israel."

"And you? What do you want?"

"I want to take Vladimir with me for now. I want to get to the camps liberated by the Americans. Sachsenhausen, Ravensbruck, and maybe Buchenwald, if you can do without me for a few days."

"You must be nuts, but I admire your courage. Why are you doing this?"

"I'm looking for my brother. The Russians burned the Jewish quarter of Brest-Litovsk to the ground. The Germans had already taken the healthy men, so Vladimir tells me, and shipped them west to the labor camps. Some of them may have survived, we think."

"I can't promise that I can give you leave, but I'll see what I can do. But I need you here tonight."

"I promise, Colonel, I'll take the best notes possible. We've heard that General Patton is expected to visit Buchenwald with General Eisenhower. Don't know how soon."

The colonel turned to Sergeant Drumm. "Sergeant, get these two cleaned up, and find them new uniforms—one without patches for Vladimir. Also get them something to eat. The corporal must be hungry; Vladimir looks starved."

"Danke schoen," Vladimir replied.

"Vladimir, the colonel is an American."

"It's okay, Corporal. Ich kann Deutsch sprechen. Vladimor, kannst du mir verstehen?"

Vladimir smiled. "Ya, Kolonel Soberman."

"I have visitors today at 1400 hours. One is my liaison from the Russian headquarters, and the other is a local German— an ex-mayor. We would like to use him to enforce new city ordinances. Both your linguistic skills will be needed tonight. Tomorrow we'll discuss other matters."

"Thank you," Vladimir managed to say. Corporal Sidowitz and Colonel Soberman shook hands.

Chapter 26

The next morning, Corporal Sidowitz and Vladimir reappeared at Colonel Soberman's headquarters. They were expected. His sanitized office was a welcome antithesis to the foul smell of the rest of the camp.

"Sit down, guys. I was very pleased with your translations last night. So were my visitors. I'm sure your German and Russian will be a great help to all of us while you're here and while you're on the road."

"Do you mean that you're giving us leave to search for survivors who may turn out to be our relatives?"

"Yes. Three days is all I can give you. You won't be able to reach the notorious camps in Poland. They are too far from Berlin. Even the Russians were shocked by what they saw there. Some tough officers were traumatized. You'll have to be satisfied with the camps closer by. But as the war was ending, the Germans moved many of the young and strong Russian inmates west to work in labor camps before they killed them. The Hebe in me still believes in miracles, so go for it.

"Provisions have been ordered for you. Sergeant Drumm has been assigned to be your driver and to keep you focused.

He'll also be watching the clock. Remember, three days … and you return here with or without finding your brother."

"Yes, sir."

"Do you have an itinerary?"

"Vladimir and I have mapped it out carefully. The closest camp is Sachenhausen, so we'll go there first. Then up to Ravensbruck, and finally Buchenwald. My mother threatens to kill herself if I don't find Yehuda or one of his children."

"While you're searching, here's a slip of paper. One of my uncles, like your brother, never came to America."

Jack took the slip of paper, scanned its contents, and put it into his pocket. "Who knows? Miracles do happen."

"By the way, I had my adjutant check the incoming mail an hour ago. Here's a pack of letters for you. Feels like it's full of news."

"And love, I hope."

Jack Sidowitz took the letters with trembling hands and waited to be dismissed. There was a lot to do to prepare for the journey to the remnants of hell.

"My Darling Jack," he read aloud, pretending to hear her voice, absorbing every stroke of her pen as if it were a gentle touch.

"A batch of letters arrived today. I knew they were from you. I cut the cord with which they had been tied together and they tumbled out, encircling me like the kisses I wanted so desperately. With eager fingers, I opened each one, read and held the words close to my heart.

"Distance had not lessened any of my feelings for you. With each letter, I love you more and cling to the hope that your hands and mouth will soon touch me as your words do now."

A single tear ran down Jack's cheek.

"Do the censors ever black out what I write to you? I hope not, though I don't know what I could say that would help the enemy. Love never started a war, but I'm unsure whether it will ever end one either.

"I am curious about Vladimir. Is he a soldier or a hungry stray who is following you around so that he can get enough to eat? Some day you'll tell me about him.

"Here in Brooklyn, there are many stars in the windows of this quiet neighborhood. Too many are gold. I am lucky to have Lota and Rubin running the business with me. Lota is studying English and has become an asset in the showroom. The buyers like her.

"Your son has grown inches since you left and gets all As in school, although it is only kindergarten. He gets handsomer every day. I show him pictures of you— the few I have—but he finds it hard to relate to the young man he hardly knew. You'll have to hone up your parenting skills when you return to me.

"'The image of your papa,' Mama Ida says to him. For a change, I agree with her.

"I wish we had conceived another child before you went overseas. It would have been a comfort to have another little Jack. We'll have to make up for it when you get home. I hope you are willing."

Jack smiled. He could not wait to release his restrained passions as soon as he could be with his beautiful Bela. It would be his pleasure to help populate the world, one child at a time. So many had died so young.

> "By the way, I have learned how to drive. Rubin got a turquoise Chevy and taught Lota and me. Although gas is rationed, Lota and I go for a ride out to Long Island sometimes on a Sunday. Your brother watches the children, and Mama Ida feeds them with homemade blintzes and other goodies. Lota and I look longingly at the models of new houses they intend to build when the soldiers return home. It could be a lovely place to raise our children.
>
> There is not enough room on this page to cover it with my most passionate love and kisses. Will send more tomorrow.
>
> Love ya, my handsome husband,
> Bela"

With a detailed map on the dashboard, Corporal Sidowitz, Vladimir, and Sergeant Drumm set off to Sachsenhausen, the nearest labor camp to Berlin. Fields of yellow-flowered rape flooded the groomed fields, waiting to be harvested and turned into canola oil. The local farmhouses were freshly painted and showed none of the ravages of war, except for an occasional broken window shutter or damaged chimney. Patches of land were devoted to growing fragrant yellow onions, and the greens of radishes were beginning to lift their crowns through the moist soil.

It seemed incredible to the trio that the prisoners on the peaks of the hill could see and smell the fruits and vegetables but could never reach out to touch or taste them. They survived on wormy black bread and old storage potatoes.

"Food was right near their fingertips!" Sergeant Drumm exclaimed.

"So why did the Germans starve us?" exploded Vladimir.

"Calm down, my friends. We will soon find out."

As they approached the camp, a train on parallel tracks abreast of the camp appeared from nowhere. It was empty. The gates to Sachsenhausen were open with the tarnished words *Arbeit Macht Frei*, copying the ominous welcome to Auschwitz, engraved on them. Two American soldiers stood guard at either end of the entrance. Sergeant Drumm handed them their orders, and after a quick glance the Americans allowed them to enter.

Corporal Sidowitz started coughing. The odor was overwhelming. Pits outside the gates smelled of rotting human flesh, and countless flies hovered above the thin layer of soil that barely camouflaged the casualties.

Vladimir jumped up in the jeep. "There," he pointed. "There's the brick factory—alongside the crematorium—where I used to work and watch as the naked children were led into the ovens while sucking on cherry lollipops! I wanted to scream out, but I didn't dare."

Corporal Sidowitz hugged him, and he sat down.

An eerie silence permeated the endless rows of bunks. As the jeep passed the mint where counterfeit currency had been printed twenty-four hours a day, a few remaining former prisoners emerged from their bunks. At first they retreated at the sight of the jeep and its uniformed service men.

Vladimir broke the silence. "Hier … Er ist Corporal Sidowitz. Er kann Deutsch and Russian sprechen." The stragglers relaxed.

An old man approached the corporal and peered at his name tag. "I knew a man called Sidor. Was the witz always there?"

"Ich gedenk nicht."

The old man limped back to his barrack.

Chapter 27

Ravensbruck was no more productive than Sachsenhausen. Outside its gates, a few German peasants were digging a mass grave for the dead victims; many laid inside the camp where they'd taken their final breaths. Under army supervision, German townspeople were collecting the corpses within the camp in wheelbarrows and bringing them out through the gates. The smell was so odious that the GIs prodded them. "Schnell, mach schneller, Deutsche."

The forced labor camp looked like any other industrial area, divided into sections for sewing, weaving, and small arms manufacturing. A special section had made V-2 robot parts for Siemens. The buildings were now empty. The German conquerors had fled when the Allies approached.

Just inside the gates, a kennel housed a dozen ferocious guard dogs that had been abandoned when the German guards escaped. They looked starved and angry, and they barked incessantly. They snarled, showing their pointed, menacing teeth, when anyone approached the cages. Suddenly, two soldiers appeared, rifles drawn, and gunned them down through the wire mesh of the kennel. The silence was welcome.

The survivors cheered. They hated the dogs, which had been

let loose, especially on small children, just for the amusement of the guards. Young women and children wandered around the blood-stained ground, scratching their infested hair and staring into space like the anorexic, dementia-stricken souls that the Nazis had turned them into.

Corporal Sidowitz felt his skin crawl and forced himself to hold back tears, and Sergeant Drumm gasped in disbelief. Vladimir showed no emotion and accepted stoically what he had seen before.

It was a humorless place. Somber American soldiers hurried through the camp setting up outdoor kitchens. A few of the healthier women offered to help them.

"Get lost," a GI yelled. "Get over to the delousing truck. It's on the north side of the hospital. There's lice all over the place. I see one crawling on your neck. Come back when you're cleaned up."

The women stepped away without arguing. They were reminded that they were untouchables.

Other survivors were lined up outside a building where two officers were registering those still able to stand erect and speak. They were issued name tags including their city of origin, whether or not those cities still existed. Some ripped off the yellow Stars of David they had been forced to wear and ground them into shreds with their feet. The threads mingled with the blood-stained earth. Others brought the stars to their lips and thanked God for keeping them alive.

An International Red Cross sign identified a former officers' club that was now being used as a hospital. There were lines there too. The stark brick building next to it had served as a mortuary and a crematorium. But no smoke was coming out of the chimney.

Sergeant Drumm tried to cheer up Jack and Vladimir. They were now on a first-name basis.

"It seems," Mike Drumm said, "more women were spared. It's rumored that the German officers liked to have sex with Jewish women."

Corporal Sidowitz glared icily at the sergeant.

Then he stepped up on a makeshift soapbox and addressed any of the survivors that would stop to listen. "*Guten Tag.* Don't be afraid. The war is ending. The Germans have been defeated. At this camp, the Americans will take care of you. Give us a little time to get better organized."

Meanwhile, Vladimir went from bunk to bunk, searching for any survivors who had been relocated from the eastern camps, especially from the area near Brest in Belarus. But he found only mothers with their babies, the offspring of female prisoners and German officers. Some were so conditioned that they could hardly remember where they had come from. They had been moved around too much.

"They did anything to stay alive, they told me," as he reported to the corporal. "Sometimes the sires threw their newborns into the fire, but sometimes they let the mothers breastfeed their children until they were older. When the babies needed more than mother's milk, they became a burden and were disposed of. Though there were many Russian women there, I met no one from Brest or other parts of Belarus."

"Well, we have one more day to look before we have to return to Berlin. Do you believe in miracles, Vladimir?"

It was the final day of their three-day pass, and Jack Sidowitz still hoped for one survivor, at least one survivor—maybe a strong young boy like Vladimir—from the city that once housed twenty thousand Jews. He had promised his mother that he would find Yehuda or one of his children they had left behind over twenty years ago. Or a grandchild, perhaps, who may even have been conceived and born in the camps.

The army cooks understood his obsession—they had all left families somewhere—and prepared sandwiches and canteens of coffee for the three of them. At five in the morning the kitchen workers packed the jeep and wished them luck. It was a five-hour trip to Buchenwald.

"Danke Schoen, auf wiedersehen." The corporal waved to the soldiers and survivors who were wandering around the camp at that early hour as he wrapped a sheaf of handwritten notes that described the conditions they had encountered so far in a waterproof folio. He had promised Colonel Soberman a report to justify granting them the three-day leave.

Colonel Soberman had given him a packet of info about Buchenwald that he was to read and share with the two others before they reached their destination near Weimar. As Sergeant Drumm drove, Corporal Sidowitz read, "Buchenwald is the most notorious forced labor and extermination camp run by the Germans inside their own country. They work their prisoners to death and believe in extermination through labor. The camp is riddled with disease and has insufficient food and unclean water. Doctors conduct inhuman medical experiments, especially on women. They use prisoners as guinea pigs to learn how much poison is needed to kill someone."

"Stop, I can't stand listening to you," Sergeant Drumm commanded.

Corporal Sidowitz ignored him.

"In April, the US Eight-Ninth Infantry overran Ohrduf, a subcamp of Buchenwald. With the impeding liberation of Buchenwald itself, the Germans initiated death marches to nowhere in an attempt to evacuate thousands from the camp, leaving the rest of the skeletons to die. They didn't have enough time to kill them all."

Vladimir vomited the sandwich he had just eaten over the side of the jeep.

"Somehow a shortwave message got to General Patton. 'This is the Buchenwald concentration camp. SOS. We request your help. They want to evacuate us. The SS wants to destroy us in one way or another.' The US Third Army responded, 'Hold out. Rushing to your aid.'

"That's all I know.

"Good luck.

"Colonel Soberman."

Sergeant Drumm pressed the accelerator to the floorboard. The jeep felt like it was flying.

Now tears ran down Corporal Sidowitz's face, and Vladimir curled up in a fetal position and sucked his thumb.

Two guard towers stood at the entrance to Buchenwald. A row of raggedy soldiers in makeshift uniforms stood on their ramps. In sync, their rifles were aimed at the trio in the jeep.

"Stop, *wie gehst du*?"

The trio raised their hands to show that they had no weapons.

"We are Americans. And you?" Jack responded.

Sergeant Drumm, to Jack's astonishment, repeated the corporal's answer in Polish. Jack learned later that the sergeant had been raised in the coalmine country of Pennsylvania, where most of his neighbors had immigrated from Eastern Europe years earlier.

"Polish resistance, rebels. We stormed the towers and showered bullets down on our captors as they fled. We're stationed here in case they try to return. One of us had a hidden short-wave transmitter when we were first brought here. He hid it so well that the Germans never found it. We reached the Third Army. An American unit is now inside the camp. Thousands died. Your medics are helping us save the ones who could not walk and were not evacuated."

An English-speaking Pole continued. "We will let you come in, but you better be who you say you are, or we will not hesitate to shoot you."

Vladimir spoke up, "Any young ones about my age survive the march here from the east, from Auschwitz?"

"A few. They cluster together in Bunk Ten. Why?"

"The corporal is looking for someone."

"Aren't we all …"

Chapter 28

Corporal Sidowitz, the linguist; Vladimir, the survivor; and Sergeant Drumm, the big Pole from Pennsylvania, an unlikely trio of companions, entered the camp. It was larger than Ravensbrook but looked just as gray, bleak, and ugly. Children with swollen bellies, their ribs pushing at their chests, surrounded the jeep, hands stretched out, begging in a multitude of languages. The soldiers had nothing but a few dozen chocolate bars to toss to them. The children scrabbled to catch the bars. Some of the older ones stole from the younger ones; some shared. The ones who managed to get a bar licked the wrapper clean after the sweet was eaten.

Vladimir took off for Bunk Ten. Sergeant Drumm engaged in a rowdy conversation with his newfound Polish buddies, and Corporal Sidowitz entered headquarters to share information about Buchenwald with the officer temporarily in charge.

Most of the soldiers, he learned, were out in the field collecting fresh produce and chickens from the disgruntled farmers; others were counting dead bodies for statistical purposes. Graves were being dug at the far corners of the camp. Army doctors were treating disease and broken bones and those liberated inmates who were still healthy and had no homes to return to.

The corporal wanted to check in with Berlin to see if there were any orders for the trio.

"Any instructions for us, Captain Elwin?"

"In fact there are. A message arrived this morning ordering me to give you a field promotion to second lieutenant when you got here."

"What? Stop foolin' around. I haven't done anything to earn it."

"That's not what Colonel Soberman thinks, and he outranks me. A reporter from *Stars and Stripes* has been shadowing your activities; he reported to the colonel that you have lifted the morale, collected information for starting functional displacement camps, and given hope to thousands. Furthermore, Colonel Soberman likes you. Of course, you're one of his kind."

"Cool it, Captain Ellis. Haven't enough of Colonel Soberman's and my kind died in the ovens?"

"Sorry, Lieutenant. Old habits die hard. I'll get one of the girls from the old sewing room to remove your stripes. Tonight after dinner, I'll pin the gold bar on your collar with a dignified short ceremony. Okay?"

"Sure."

As Jack Sidowitz left headquarters, Vladimir came running toward him, trailed by a frail girl with long legs. She was undernourished and underdeveloped, but her eyes looked old. There were sores on her arms and legs. On her threadbare, washed-out dress that had once been blue, she wore a name tag: "Mosha Vinkovsky—Brest-Litovsk."

Jack froze. He held his out hand to her, but she pulled hers away. Was she afraid that he would smack or molest her?

"Don't be afraid, little girl. I'm an American. I left Russia a long time ago. Coincidently, I once lived in the city of

Brest-Litovsk." The new lieutenant continued. "Your father doesn't happen to be called Yehuda?"

She nodded, but her eyes remained sad.

"Is it possible that you are my brother's grandchild?"

A flood of tears flowed from her sad eyes and covered her face. "Papa, Mama—do you know where they are?"

"Not yet. Do you know where they are?"

"My brother and sister are dead; so is Mikol, my sister's baby boy. I saw them marched naked into the gas chambers, but they never walked out. Their dead bodies were moved to the crematorium and burned. I could see the smoke come out of the chimney from the window of the ice-cold building where I was sewing uniforms. I wanted to run toward them and die with them, but the fat matron slammed me across the legs with her club. She wouldn't let me out of the locked factory."

"Why were you spared?"

"I'm a good seamstress. Gold embroidered emblems had to be sewn on the officers' uniforms with almost invisible stitches. While I sewed, the soldiers laughed as they watched the naked prisoners walk to their death."

"My brother Yehuda was the only Vinkovsky in Brest. You must be his grandchild—my niece."

"Grandpa talked about his brothers in America. Are you one of them?"

"I'm Jacov—Jack in American. Let me hold you close and comfort you. Now that I've been promoted, maybe I can make arrangements to get you out of here when I return to Berlin. Be patient. The war will be over very soon, and I will figure out how to get you to America. Your grandmother is waiting to love and care for you."

"I don't trust anyone in uniform. Are you telling the truth?"

Vladimir broke in. "This is your uncle, the best soldier I

have ever met. He loves you. You'd better tell him about our other plans."

"You tell him, Vladimir. You planned it all."

"Mosha, I, and the few others who are still healthy enough will try to get to Italy. A camp there is the closest one to Israel."

"How?"

"We'll hike, climb over mountains, hop on trains moving south. We'll swim rivers and steal food if we have to. We'll do anything except pray. We did that for very long, but it did us no good. If we survived the camps, we can survive anywhere. Mosha is sixteen but looks twelve because she has been so mistreated and underfed. She will be lovely one day after I get her to a safe place. I need to love someone in order to live and give life. I'll take good care of her, I promise."

"Why don't I get permission to take Mosha back to Berlin with us?" Jack asked. "Both of you need to grow stronger, gain a little weight, maybe rethink this dangerous journey. The fields are full of mines, and the woods hide vengeful Nazis who still want to murder us. The rickety ships for hire taking survivors to Palestine are being blown out of the waters by the cannons of British destroyers that block the entrances to Palestine ports."

"Sorry, Jack, or Lieutenant Sidowitz. I respect you, and I love you like a brother, but we leave tonight. Please give me your address in America."

Part 4

Chapter 29

O n the last day of April, the Germans garnered all their strength and tried to turn back the Allied offensive, but the American air power in the Battle of Berlin almost totally destroyed the city. Rather than surrender, Adolph Hitler and his mistress committed suicide. Three days later, the German forces in Italy laid down their arms.

In the first week of May, Jack worked twenty-four hours a day, seven days a week, simultaneously translating negotiations between the German generals and Colonel Soberman and his Russian counterpart, Colonel Georgi Kerokov. Berlin was in shambles. The remaining soldiers in the city had laid down their arms, although in outer pockets of the country fierce fighting often continued. Sergeant Drumm had gone back to his other duties. Jack had no time to think about either Vladimir or his lovely wife Bela back in New York.

The highlight of his assignment was to translate the German Instrument of Surrender before it was signed on May 7.

"Hi, Lieutenant Sidowitz!" A cheery new draftee entered Jack's office. "I'm from the mail room. I just got here from the States. It's so exciting! Sergeant Drumm asked me to bring this letter to you personally."

Jack nonchalantly replied, "Thanks, Private."

Jack could tell from the handwriting on the envelope that it was from Bela. With trembling hands, he carefully opened the onion-skin v-mail envelope, held it to his lips for a moment, and scanned the sheet with its tabs. For a masthead, Bela had sketched a picture of an adoring mother hugging a little boy. Jack smiled at the images of his family, as if he could see them. He began to read aloud.

My love, my darling, she wrote.

They tell us in America that the war in Europe is ending. Hopefully you will be coming home soon. I can hardly wait to hold you in my arms.

Every street is planning a block party with balloons, favors, and swing music for dancing. A few soldiers and sailors have been discharged early probably, because they suffered critical wounds, but we are anxiously awaiting the return of all of you. I'm on the entertainment committee, and Mama Ida is on the food committee. She's baking your favorite cakes already and freezing them in the Italian restaurant that opened on the corner while you were away.

Our son walks now and says Mama and Dada, but he thinks Uncle Rubin is his father. Ruby and Lota have been so good to us, but I miss you more every day.

I know that you are a brilliant linguist, but please don't learn Japanese, or they'll send you off to the Pacific. I couldn't bear your absence much longer. You are older than the boys being shipped out to Europe now, and it's time they replaced you. I need your arms around me in the big bed and another baby in my belly.

I went to the post office today and found out how to send a package and photographs to you. I knitted the argyle socks myself to keep your feet warm. As long as you are in a permanent base, you can receive mail.

By the way, what happened to Vladimir? A letter arrived for you from Italy, but Rubin can't read Russian. Do we know anyone who was sent to Italy?

Jack yelled out, "It's from Vladimir. He's reached Italy alive, I know it. Oh, God. Keep Mosha safe."

Alarmed by his outburst, everyone in the offices turned to look at Jack

"Lieutenant, are you all right?" the private asked.

"Fine. Just surprised that there can be good news somewhere in the world. You're dismissed. I've got work to do."

The young private left the office, and Jack returned to reading Bela's letter.

Rubin will go to shul with Mama on Saturday and have the rabbi translate the letter into English, and I'll send the original and the translation on to you.

Your brothers are coming over for dinner on Shabbat. Louis is making a bundle from manufacturing shoulder pads for the army. His brother-in-law financed him and is a silent partner. Nathan has taken over the gas station for himself, and now that more gas is being delivered, he is also all making big dollars. We expect that women will want beautiful things to wear when the war ends. Our belts will be a desirable accessory, and Belabelts will prosper with you out there selling.

By the way, Mama is growing frail and forgetful. We haven't told her anything about Mosha because we don't

*want to give her false hopes. On WEVD, HIAS reads
the names of released camp prisoners who are looking
for relatives in America. She keeps hearing the name
Yehuda and sends Rubin down to HIAS every week to
see if it is her Yehuda, but it never is. She buys the* Daily
Forward *every day, and the butcher reads to her about
something the papers are calling concentration camps,
saying that so many Jews were killed, or gassed, as they
say. What do they mean by gassed?*

Jack decided not to explain until he was home and holding
Bela in his arms.

*That's my red lipstick on the four corners of this
letter. Please come home in one piece, my love, so I can
plant my love on your lips.*
Always yours,
Bela

Letter still in hand, Lieutenant Sidowitz walked into Colonel
Soberman's office.

"Good afternoon, sir."

"What can I do for you, Lieutenant?"

"Colonel, when can I go home? I'm afraid my wife is
breaking down, my business is suffering, and my son is calling
my brother daddy. At least I need a leave. I can't continue at this
pace. Don't you ever feel that way?"

"I once did, but my wife left me for the deferred owner of
a shipping company that's making a ton of dollars from this
war; the children are in college, and I'm regular army. I might
as well stay here."

"I'm sorry, sir."

"Not your fault, Lieutenant." The colonel sighed. "I hate to do without you, but we're getting a batch of new recruits right out of Ivy League colleges. They majored in languages, especially Russian, so they'll be a great help. They should be arriving next week. I need you to train them. It should take about two to three weeks. During that time, I'll see what I can do. R&R on the Riviera might be possible, but a trip home … that's a long shot."

"Funny, I never thought of myself as a teacher, but training sounds like a good experience. Not sure I want to sell belts at Belabelts for the rest of my life when I get home. I'll let my brother and wife handle the business and go back to school. I hear the GI Bill will pay for it. War does some strange things to men."

"And women," added the colonel.

Chapter 30

A dozen baby-faced soldiers arrived in Berlin a week after Lieutenant Jack Sidowitz's conversation with the colonel. Their Russian and German sounded like they had just graduated from a university. It was Jack's job to make their speech more casual so that they could mingle with the Russian soldiers and the German civilians in the cafes and on the street. Lieutenant Sidowitz was a good teacher.

Jack counted each day before he returned to the States to his dear Bela and young son.

On a rainy Tuesday three weeks later, he entered Colonel Soberman's headquarters. The private at the desk outside his office saluted.

"I'm Lieutenant Sidowitz, Private. Is the colonel in?"

"Yes, sir. In fact, he's been looking for you. I didn't know if you were still upstairs teaching the new batch of interpreters. He said if you came by to just knock and go in, sir."

Jack did as he was told and was greeted by a smiling colonel.

"Great news, Lieutenant. Your seven-day R&R has been approved. You and a group of five other soldiers are heading for the Hotel-du-Cap-Eden Roc—"

"*Great*! You're wonderful! Bela can fly down to Florida and meet me there. Maybe she'll bring my son. I don't know how to thank you."

"Hold it, Lieutenant. The Eden Roc is a hotel in Antibes, on the French Riviera, as close to the Mediterranean as you can get. First you'll be flown to Paris for two days. Then you and the others will take a train to Nice, where a truck will pick you up at the station and take you to the Eden Roc."

Jack's face fell. "You mean I'm not going home?"

"Don't look so glum. Paris chose to be an open city during the war, so the Eiffel Tower and its other monuments were hardly damaged. Despite the cowardly French who wouldn't fight against the Germans to defend Paris, they might have done us a favor. You'll be overwhelmed by its beauty."

"I guess so."

"Don't be disheartened. The war's over. The army's discharging men every day. Maybe the next step will be an honorable discharge for you, and you'll go home for good.

In the summer of 1945, while Jack Sidowitz was on R&R on the French Riviera, unless he had been secretly transferred to the Pacific, soldiers started returning home from the European Theater operations.

Bela and Lota had joined the Seventy-Fifth Street Association in Brooklyn and were planning a block party for the servicemen returning from Europe. They hesitated, because many of the neighborhood boys were still fighting in the Pacific Theater. There was talk of an invasion of Japan.

Rubin, who had not gone to war, was now a successful businessman. He offered to pay for any homecomings his wife and sister-in-law planned. The belt business had been good, and contributing to these celebrations made him feel less guilty that he had not served his country in uniform. He had bought a generous number of Victory bonds.

In the kitchen of Rubin and Lota's house, Bela hugged her brother-in-law. "Oh Rubin, you've been so generous to us, but can't we wait to celebrate until Jack gets back?

"No word from him yet?"

"No. I'm sure we'll hear something any day now. After all, he's a father and older than a lot of the younger soldiers—maybe the army considers that when they release men."

"My brother, a Russian immigrant, is an officer in the United States Army. I'm so proud."

Shabbat was always open house at Lota and Rubin's house.

A neighbor rang the bell.

"Enter," Rubin called out, unwilling to get up from his seat at the table. Lota had just served hot tea from a silver samovar that Rubin had bought Lota for her last birthday, and Russian pastries, dipped in honey to conserve sugar, waited on the table.

A balding man with a potbelly wearing a City College sweatshirt barged in and went straight to Rubin.

"Hi, old friend. We don't see you around anymore. You're the only one on the block with the latest Studebaker, and your brother, Nathan, makes sure you have enough gas, rationing or not. Have you gotten too rich to associate with us?" said his old friend Stanley.

"Don't be *narish*. You know, silly I mean. The economy is booming. We're working two shifts so we can fill the orders from Macy's and B. Altman's. American women want to dress up for their husbands when they come home. I'm so busy I hardly get home, except to sleep."

"But some husbands won't ever come home, and others who were mustered out can't find jobs. My son Marty, the one with the pregnant wife, was wounded by the Germans and is being discharged from the VA hospital next week."

"Can he sew?"

"I don't know, but he learned to be a pattern-maker at the Fashion Industries High School before he went to war. If he could learn to shoot, I'm sure he can learn to sew."

Rubin smiled at his neighbor. "Okay, send him to see me when he gets home. If we like each other I'll let one of the new girls go. Her boyfriend's being discharged at the end of the month, and she's getting married and moving to Georgia."

"Georgia? What for?"

"His father has a prosperous used car–parts business in Atlanta. All the old cars on the road are falling apart. He's waiting for his son to take over so he can retire. All the girls talk about in the shop is getting married."

"Sounds good to me. Thanks, Rubin. Marty has an artificial leg, but he's got a great pair of hands. He'll be a good worker. Maybe in a few years, he can buy one of Mr. Levitt's houses for veterans. Imagine, ninety dollars down and forty-five dollars a month."

"I hear this Mr. Levitt is a genius. The houses will have a carport, a garden, and two or three bedrooms … just like we had in Russia, where we all slept in one bed."

Marty chimed in. "It was the only way to keep warm during a Russian winter."

They could hear the children playing in the backyard, laughing and yelling to each other.

"Catch the ball before it goes over the fence."

"Mrs. Doyle will keep it. She never gives them back. She saves them for her own grandchildren."

"Then let's play Three Feet to Germany. She's too old to catch us!" shouted the oldest.

"Keep quiet!" Bela yelled out the window.

"Calm down, Bela," Lota chimed in. "It must be safe. The mayor has cancelled all future air raid drills until further notice."

The children lowered their voices.

She and Lota had been listening to the conversation between Rubin and his friend from the kitchen.

"I wonder what it's like having a husband with a missing limb."

"It makes me shudder. Please change the subject. I've starting baking cookies for the block party, and I've saved enough coffee cans to store them in so they'll be fresh whenever we need them. But I've run out of butter. Do you have any ration stamps left, Bela?"

"I think so."

Bela went off to the bedroom and came back with the ration book she had pushed into the back of her pocketbook.

"Here, take what you need. Smile at Mr. Schwartz. He likes you better than me. Maybe he'll throw in an extra quarter pound."

Lota took her purse from the cabinet, grabbed a purple sweater from a hook in the foyer, and dashed out the door, almost knocking over the mailman.

"Oops," she said. "Maybe you have something good for us today." Before waiting for an answer, she continued to the corner grocery store.

Lota returned with a grin on her face. Mr. Schwartz had thrown in some extra butter when she told him what it was for. Before going upstairs, she looked in her bag for the mailbox key. It was not there.

She hurried up to the apartment, dropped the butter on the

kitchen table, found the key in the pocket of the apron she had forgotten to take off when she left the house, and returned to the mailbox.

There it was, a picture postcard of the village of Camogli, with its boardwalk, hotels, and fishing boats and the seawall that separated the harbor from the Mediterranean. Jack had written, "I have seen so much ugliness, but the world can be beautiful. Maybe it will be some day. Kiss Mama and Bela for me. Love, Jack."

Lota dashed back upstairs. "Bela, Rubin, Marty's father, listen!" she shouted. She read the words on the back of the card to them.

"Bela," she almost ordered, "run home. I bet there's a letter from Jack waiting for you."

Bela wiped her hands on a dish towel and ran out the door.

"Hey," Rubin yelled after her, "take a sweater. It's cold outside."

Bela ignored her brother-in-law's advice. She fled out into the street and down the block to her apartment.

There was no mail.

Upstairs, shedding a river of tears, she picked up the silver frame containing the photograph of Jack in a lieutenant's uniform, looking at her with his big brown eyes. The tears dwindled to an occasional sob as she kissed his lips, moistening the photograph. Then she heard a key in the door.

"Who is it?" she shouted, a little afraid.

Before she could catch her breath or scream, there he stood, her Jack, tanned from the Mediterranean sun, officers' bars on his shoulder, a few gray hairs in the wavy crown of his brown/black hair and at his temples, just as handsome as ever. There were no words between them, just two pairs of arms reaching out to each other, holding, stroking, clinging, shedding their clothes, colors mingling with designs and decorations, leaving a trail that reached into the bedroom.

A while later, Bela whispered to him, "I've missed you so much."

"I love you, my darling. Every day in that land of death, I hung on to your love. It gave me the will to live."

She was so glad that Mama Ida had taken Little William to the zoo.

Chapter 31

When Bela didn't return to Rubin and Lota's house, her relatives began to worry. Although they were one of the lucky families who had a phone, it was a party line, and every time Lota tried to call Bela, she found herself listening to Mrs. Goldberg's conversation with her daughter.

"Where could she have gone?" Rubin asked.

"I don't know. Maybe you should run down the block and see if everything is all right?"

"She's a grown American woman. There are no pogroms in Brooklyn."

"I know, Ruby, but I'm feeling uneasy."

"Uneasy, schmeasy, but I'll go. Get me my jacket."

After Rubin left, Lota turned on the radio in the kitchen and tuned into her favorite station, WEVD. She loved to hear Yiddish: the unique warmth of the language, descriptions of peasants like her dead mother and father, life in the shtetl, Chasidim dancing in the Polish village square, and the cantor singing in the wooden synagogue that she had heard from a recent arrival had been burned down by the Germans. When the singing ended, HIAS, the Hebrew Immigration Aid Society, took to the air.

"Good evening, friends and relatives. Welcome to another evening of hope. A HIAS mission has just returned from Europe after visiting what are now called displaced camps. The men, women, and children who survived the German brutality were being fed and clothed by humanitarian groups and the armed forces of several nations. Many are looking for relatives in the United States. From now on, HIAS will record and broadcast the names of those survivors every Sunday night at seven. Here's our first list.

"Cohen, Schmuel, looking for Tante Fredle Geldmeister from Brooklyn.

"Zweig, Miriam, looking for brother, Samuel Zweig in Cleveland.

"Rudofskov, Emil, looking for the famous professor Dr. Solomon Rudofsky on the East Coast."

And then, as she continued ironing Ruby's shirts, she heard it. "Vinkovsky, Mosha, separated from her husband-to-be, Vladimir Sornoff, who might now be in Palestine; looking for grandmother Ida Sidowitz or her sons in Brooklyn, New York."

Lota momentarily froze where she stood at the ironing board.

The announcer continued. "If you recognize someone's name, come down to the HIAS offices at 425 Lafayette Street and ask to see Fred Wolfson or Golda Greenhouse. Bring any identity papers or photographs of the survivor and yourself with you. It will help us make a connection. Tune in next Sunday for the names of more survivors looking for relatives."

A Yiddish melody concluded the broadcast.

Lota's face grew warm as her cheeks flushed; she felt her blood pressure rise. She put down the iron and disconnected the cord. Was it possible that Yehuda or any of his children or grandchildren had survived the massacres that the Nazis had committed?

She would send Rubin down to the HIAS office Monday morning. First she had to ask mama what Yehuda's last name was. It was not Sidowitz, as his father was Ida's first husband. She was sure that her mother-in-law had saved some early letters from her eldest son when they first arrived in America. Nathan, who had had some schooling in Russia, had read them to Ida; the rabbi had answered them for her. She had never heard Rubin, Jack, or Mama Ida call the eldest anything but Yehuda.

Lota paced up and back in the kitchen. First she tried calling Bela's house. Mrs. Goldberg was still on the party line phone.

"Why isn't Rubin back yet?" she asked herself.

Rubin knocked. No one answered. He thought he heard the sound of heavy breathing and then an ecstatic cry. Still no one answered. He pounded harder on Bela's door, shouting, "Bela, Bela, open the door! Are you all right?"

A male voice finally shouted back, "Ruby, *geh awek* – get lost. I'm home for a few days. I haven't had my wife for months. Bela's excited; so am I."

Then Ruby heard Bela moan contentedly.

Jack continued. "Tell Lota I'll stop at the house later, maybe tomorrow. Although I'm aching to see my son, ask Mama to keep William overnight. Make up a reason if you have to. I've dreamed about Bela every night in that wretched place they call Germany. This wonderful night mustn't end. But don't let Mama know that I'm home. I want to surprise her."

"Why didn't you stop at our house first? The family was all together an hour ago."

"Jack, tell Ruby to go away," Bela moaned again.

"Lota received a picture postal card from you, so Bela ran

home to check her mail. We were so worried about her when she didn't come back."

"I was glad to find her alone, so cut the conversation. Can't you hear her sighing?"

"Are you all right, brother?"

"Me? Okay. My body's whole, and my arms and legs are healthy. Now I have my gorgeous wife in my arms. Go home. You'll look me over later when we come by."

Rubin smiled, shook his head, and ran down the front steps. Jacob, now Lieutenant Jack Sidowitz, had always been a lady's man.

Sunlight streamed through the venetian blinds on Sunday morning, illuminating her naked shoulders, but Bela made no attempt to get out of bed to pick up the clothes and underwear scattered all over the bedroom. Jack lay on his stomach, one arm across his wife's midsection, staring at her placid face, pleased that he had given her pleasure. He glanced at the clock radio.

"Honey ..." He slid his fingers between her full breasts and whispered in her ear, "Does Rubin still have family breakfasts on Sunday morning?"

She nodded her head in assent.

"I think we have to get up now. It's time to say hello to Lota and my brothers. It's time to hug Mama and welcome my son William. He must be a big, little boy by now. I'm not even sure that he'll recognize me."

"Of course he will. I've shown him pictures, and I've told him so much about you. But do we have to go now?"

"They'll be other nights, many nights, I promise you."

"How long can you stay?"

"Didn't I tell you? I'm being discharged next Friday at Fort Dix, New Jersey. Next Shabbat, I'll be a civilian again. I'm here, back in America forever."

Bela rolled over on top of him, rubbing her body against his until he responded.

"Oh, I'm so happy, Jack darling. I can't get enough of you. Once more, my love, before we shower and dress."

By eleven forty-five, Bela and Jack, radiant in their contentment, were ringing Rubin and Lota's bell. They had noticed Louis's and Nathan's cars parked in front of the house. A Welcome Back Jack sign was on the door, and excited voices were coming from inside. The door was unlocked, so the couple walked right in.

Everyone tried to hug Jack at once. The women cried tears of joy. Little William began to cry when Jack picked him up. But when he decided to play with the silver bar on his father's uniform, the crying subsided.

Mama stood in a corner looking at the joyous homecoming but not joining in the festivities. With his son in his arms, Jack approached his mother. Little William seemed relieved to find the familiar figure of this grandmother there. They hugged and kissed, and the old woman cried as she examined Jack to make sure he had all his limbs. The others watched with smiles on their faces.

On the white linen tablecloth were all the foods that Jack liked and hadn't eaten since he had been inducted into the army. There was a silvery herring, lox, smoked sable, and ripe red tomatoes. There were radishes and pickled cucumbers. The sliced red onion earned its own plate, as the children didn't like the smell. A long, twisted raisin challah sat in the center of the table, surrounded by various kinds of bagels for those who preferred that kind of bread.

Rubin chanted, "*Baruch atah*. Thank God we are altogether."

Chapter 32

reakfast was a lively affair. The older children kept the younger ones busy with the toy trains that Rubin had brought home. Their parents hugged and kissed each other but gave most of their attention to Jack. Bela and her husband sat next to each other, holding hands under the white linen tablecloth. The whole family talked at once, hardly giving their hero a chance to answer.

"Tell us about Berlin."

"Who is Vladimir?"

"Did you visit the camps?"

"Did you get to Brest-Litovsk?"

"What was it like going to Dartmouth? I hope my son can go there someday."

"Are you being discharged?"

"Belabelts needs you. Business is booming."

Jack was overwhelmed by the questions and answered only in monosyllabic sentences.

Rubin bailed him out. "There's lots of time for Jack to answer all those questions. Right now we have serious business, and we need Mama's help."

Everyone stopped talking.

"Lota heard a survivor's name—a girl looking for the Sidowitz family—on the HIAS radio program. She calls herself Mosha Vinkovsky. But we can't remember Yehuda's last name! I need to know at least that before I go down to HIAS tomorrow morning. Jack, do you know anything about his family?"

"Not much. Events and information were sometimes a little blurred during the war. I met an emaciated young girl at one of the camps who said her name was Mosha Vinkovsky, and she came from Brest. She said she'd seen her parents murdered and the city burned, and then she covered her body in its thin cotton dress with her hands and ran back into her barracks. Vladimir, the young Russian boy who became my tail, befriended her. He came from Vinograd, a town near Brest. Even in that squalor, a romance blossomed. When she was healthy enough to leave camp they fled to Italy so that they could possibly get to Palestine. Most of the young Jews wanted to go there."

Mama muttered under her breath. "Vinkovsky, Vinkovsky … I had the rabbi read the last letter from Yehuda before the Germans invaded Russia to me. But where, where did I put it? I know I saved it, and the envelope too. The stamp had a picture of the Leningrad Cathedral on it, before the Communists made it a museum."

"Maybe it's in your sewing box. I've seen you put things in there." Lota jumped up. "Let me help you find it."

"I'll help too," said Bela, letting go of Jack's hand.

"Maybe Lota heard wrong and it was not Vinkovsky," Louis's wife interjected.

"Keep still, Esther. You don't know what you're talking about."

"I'm so nervous, my hands are shaking." Mama ignored her oldest daughter-in-law. "Come, girls, I can't do it alone. Let's go to my apartment. We'll turn the dresser drawers upside down, my pocketbooks inside out. It's got to be somewhere. I would never have thrown his letters away."

Rubin and Jack exchanged glances. Nathan broke the silence. "If she's really Yehuda's grandchild and you need money to get her out of Europe, Louis and I will give it to you."

"I wonder what happened to Vladimir? He really loved her. Maybe they even married," Jack mused aloud to his brothers. "In the short time I was there, many couples married in the camp."

"Maybe he got to Israel without her and then left her. It happens all the time in America. Your Uncle Paul left a wife in Russia to come to America and never sent for her."

"Or maybe he was killed when he tried to swim ashore from an old merchant ship."

"Maybe the ship was attacked by the British as they sneaked across the Mediterranean," Louis chimed in.

Jack grew angry. "Stop fantasizing. You don't know anything about the way the camps were! I'm sorry, Louis. Vladimir helped me throughout Germany. He was like a teenage son with the wisdom of an old man who had cunningly survived the camps."

"I'm sorry, Jack," Louis said. "I didn't mean to upset you. Will you be home long enough to help us locate Mosha?"

"I'm being discharged on Friday. Until then, all my time belongs to my darling Bela and my son I like to call Willie. And I don't want to go back to work at the belt factory for a while. I need to pinch myself every morning in the big bed beside Bela to feel alive. After a few weeks, I'll start to think about my future and the choices I have."

Again the brothers exchanged glances.

"Of course, I'll help, Ruby. Louis, Nathan, just be ready with the money if we need some."

At that moment the door burst open. Mama, Bela, and Lota rushed in. Mama was waving a letter at them. *"Ich habe es gefunden*; I found it! My first husband's name was Vinkovsky. I even found my first marriage papers. Will that help prove to HIAS that we are not kidnapping her, that she is one of us?"

"Jack, maybe tomorrow morning, we should take Mama with us."

By eight thirty the next morning, Mama, dressed in her best Shabbat navy suit, its white jabot enhancing her long neck, sat at the kitchen table waiting for her sons. She carried a red folder containing all the personal papers and photographs of her family she had treasured on the voyage and upon her arrival in America.

Still half asleep, Rubin shuffled into the kitchen, clean-shaven and dressed like he was going to a business meeting.

"Coffee, Reuven?"

"No, Mama, thanks."

Ida still liked to call her sons by their Hebrew names every so often.

Moments later, using his old key, Jack walked into the apartment, straight, tall, and distinguished in his lieutenant's uniform.

"Are we ready? Driving or taking the train, Rubin?"

"I think Mama will be more comfortable in my car. Let's go."

Rubin drove down to Lafayette Street, where new HIAS headquarters had been enlarged. An outdated federal office had been remodeled to house it. A long line had already formed around the building; the Sidowitzes joined the queue.

A babble of languages—Yiddish, Italian, Greek, Hungarian, and others—infiltrated the air. Everyone was clutching papers in overstuffed boxes, and ragged folders. From every displaced nationality, these were the relatives who were hoping to enter America, although the recent restriction laws had lowered the quotas for Eastern Europeans, making it nearly impossible for the Poles and Russians who had arrived here years ago to bring in the remnants of their families who had been left behind. The German-speaking Americans remained quiet.

Jack was restless. He walked up and down alongside the line, stopping frequently near Rubin and Mama to give them encouragement. A well-dressed middle-aged lady wearing a HIAS badge that identified her as Rebecca Stein approached him.

"Are you a veteran, Lieutenant?" Mrs. Stein asked.

"Yes, Mrs. Stein. My name is Jack Sidowitz, Lieutenant Jack Sidowitz."

"Why are you here?"

"I was in Germany when the war ended, and I believe I found my brother's granddaughter in a DP camp."

"Was she young?"

"Maybe sixteen. She was wearing a tag that read 'Mosha Vinkovsky, Brest-Litovsk.' She was transported west from Russia to a work camp outside of Berlin."

"How did you know?"

"Something about her made me suspicious. Her big brown eyes underneath long lashes peered at me from her bony face like her father's used to do when I didn't bring in the wood or milk the cow. But when I immigrated to America from that city with my family, my eldest brother chose to stay behind. His children were married, and a grandchild was expected. He was sure that the impending war would pass over. After the Germans invaded Russia we never heard from him again.

"I was drafted, and to my surprise I was trained to be an interpreter for the US Army. My commanding officer, Colonel Soberman, gave me a three-day pass to look for any family survivors in the camps near Berlin. He let me take Vladimir, a Russian youth who had survived several work camps and knew his way around one camp to another. The colonel was not optimistic that we would find anyone, but Vladimir actually did."

"Where is she now?"

"I don't know. When the Allies opened the gates, she and the young Russian boy, Vladimir, walked out of the camp with a flood of other young ones and headed for Italy—a camp near Bari—and then maybe, if they were lucky, on a boat to Palestine. Once the gates of the camps were opened, the survivors could go anywhere they wanted to. There was no formal plan for what to do with them, and most had no home to go back to."

"HIAS has an office in Italy. Did you know that it coordinates activities with the US Consul?"

"I didn't even know what HIAS was all about until I got home last week. My sister-in-law listens to WEVD. She thinks she heard Mosha's name; and that she was looking for relatives in New York. That's why I'm here. Lota came to America as an orphan after World War I and knows a lot more than I do about the Hebrew Immigration Aid Society. Can you help us find Mosha?"

"Why didn't she stay with you in Berlin? Because you are a soldier, the US Consul General's office might have helped you, especially since she is so young."

"Me? Juliet had found her Romeo in the depths of hell."

"I'm a softie, Lieutenant. You remind me of my only son, who was shot down over Germany in '43. Gather your family, and I'll try to get you in before the others. There are not too many veterans on this line."

Jack collected Rubin and Mama, and they followed Mrs. Stein.

"Hey, you in the uniform—we're ahead of you," a burly Irishman yelled.

Jack pretended not to hear.

Mrs. Stein yelled back, "Hold your horses. You'll all be seen, even if we have to work until midnight. This man fought in Europe and helped open the DP camps. Haven't you read about the horrors over there in the newspapers and seen them on the Movietone newsreels?"

Once inside the stained walls of the building, the family was overwhelmed by the frantic activity, the cacophony of voices, the screams of elation, and the sobs of despair. Mrs. Stein led the way and ushered them into the office of Mr. R. Brenner, examiner. Mrs. Stein gave the examiner a brief synopsis of her conversation with Jack and left the room.

"Welcome home, Lieutenant. Now let's get down to business. First: name of the relative and relationship?"

"Mosha Vinkovsky, niece"

"If her grandfather or father was your brother, why isn't her name Sidowitz?"

"Her great-grandfather, was our mother's first husband."

At that moment Mama stood up, her dark eyes blazing, and scowled at Mr. Brenner. She pulled out her papers, pointed a finger at Mr. Brenner, who almost fell off his chair, and spread them all over his desk.

"See, my first marriage certificate: Groom: Schlomo Vinkovsky, age twenty-one. Here's his death certificate. Killed by a Cossack he was. We had only one son together. His name was Yehuda, and he kept his father's surname. No other family in the village was named Vinkovsky, and now my granddaughter carries that name. She must be part of our family, maybe the only one who survived."

"Please, Mrs. Sidowitz, let me ask the questions."

Jack and Rubin were stunned. They had not known that their mother had absorbed so much English in the years that they had been in America.

"And you are her uncles, I presume?"

"Yes, we are," said Rubin.

"Can you support her?"

"Of course. We have two other brothers, and we all have good businesses in America. We can pay her passage if necessary."

"If she's under eighteen and an orphan, HIAS might speed things up and pay for her passage, so don't worry. But first we have to find her."

"The only letter we got from her was from Cine Citta, an Italian DP camp near Genoa. It was as close to Israel as she and Vladimir could get. Broken-down boats from Greece and Italy tried to sneak past the British warships blockading Palestine, but only a few succeeded. Most were returned to their port of departure."

"Lots of displaced persons married when they were freed. Can you finance both of them if they are married?"

"I'm sure we can"

"Would it be easier to get them here if, perhaps, she is pregnant?" Rubin said.

"What makes you think so?" asked Mr. Brenner.

"Loneliness."

"We'll see," Mr. Brenner replied.

"Look up Belabelts Company, Inc. We can get you all the necessary references, including the New York City Chamber of Commerce and the Ladies Garment Workers Union. Do you need to know where we bank?" Rubin exclaimed.

"Premature, but I admire your spirit, all three of you." The examiner smiled.

"Would Mosha come alone?" he continued.

"We don't know if she or Vladimir made it to Israel. We would have to ask them if they want to come to America. But if Mosha is looking for us, she certainly is considering it. It's funny. I thought I told Vladimir how to reach us in the United States, but we've moved since then," added Jack.

"If they married, there would be no problem bringing them both, but the wait between visas and transportation to the United States is long. Not too many ships are sailing back and forth yet, certainly not with our right-wing American Congress afraid of Jewish immigration and a president consumed with how to defeat Japan."

Jack was shocked, but Mr. Brenner's secretary didn't give him time to absorb the examiner's last statement. She took him into a small adjoining office. There they filled out numerous forms and affidavits to help trace Mosha's whereabouts before HIAS could even attempt to procure a visa for their niece and bring her in as an under-age child.

When Jack returned to Mr. Brenner's office, Mama had collected her papers. She stood up and straightened her skirt.

"We'll be in touch," Mr. Brenner said. "We'll get busy tracing Mosha's whereabouts through our European connections. If you don't hear from me in two weeks, one of you should call. I'll have more news by then. Will you still be in New York, Lieutenant Sidowitz?"

"I think so. Discharge day is Friday, and it's not a wedding ceremony! Thanks for everything, Mr. Brenner."

"Thank Mrs. Stein on the way out. You remind her of her son. He was a great young man and was engaged to my daughter."

Chapter 33

It was a week after Jack was discharged from the army, and he still hadn't heard from Mr. Brenner, but he remained patient. He enjoyed sleeping late in the mornings with his arms around Bela and playing with his son as they began to get to know each other. In quieter moments Jack thought about his future.

He spent a day at the Belabelt factory, which now had forty employees, many of them refugees. He was proud of what his brother Rubin, his wife, and Bela had done, yet he knew, despite the company's success, that he didn't want to spend his life there. Jack could sell, fire a weapon, and speak several languages. He had an urge to join the clandestine groups of pro-Israel ex-soldiers to help the survivors get to their homeland, since no one else wanted them.

Restless, he wandered down to the Brooklyn piers one afternoon and ran into Nick Ascaro, who had recently been discharged from the navy. Nick had taken part in the invasion of Italy and had been privy to opening an Italian detention camp full of frantic Jews eager to get to Palestine. The son of Italian immigrants, Nick had gone to night school with Jack before they both went into service, and he was a restless spirit too. He was also the nephew of a Mafia capo on the waterfront.

"Nick, remember me?"

"Sure do. You and your brother hung out at Dave's candy store, waiting for the phone to ring so you could fetch someone on the block waiting for a call who was also a big tipper.

"You're the yid with the glib tongue. You could sell the Brooklyn Bridge, even with your accent. How'd you get rid of it?"

"Believe it or not, the army sent me to language school. I now speak German, Russian, some Polish, Yiddish, and English, of course. But they didn't think I was romantic enough to learn Italian."

Nick laughed. "I heard your brother made a big success out of your belt business while you were gone. Are you going back into the business?"

"Not yet. Not interested in selling belts and not ready to register for college, at least not until the fall. I've got a yen for education, as long as the United States is buying. What about you?"

"Have a wife who fooled around while I was away and a son I'm not sure is mine, so I'm restless."

"Didn't the family keep an eye on her?"

"I guess not, or she wouldn't be around anymore."

"Did you get to know any of the Jews in the DP camps in Italy?"

"Yeah, my street Yiddish from hanging with you guys came in handy. It was just like the pictures in the newspapers … Sick, forsaken, fragile beings without families; ashamed to be alive; not wanting to die. The camps in Italy were not as painful. There was enough to eat, and the local nuns were bringing clothes for those walking around half naked."

"Would expect that of the Italians. They never wanted this war in the first place."

"Some of those in the camps are getting money from abroad and will pay anything to get out of Italy and slip past the British blockade to where the Palmach picks them up and gets them to Palestine.

"Uncle Tony tells me that the Italian banks are still functioning, and he has dozens of connections in Genoa. He needs a few tough men to load the boats, hide the passengers below deck, and navigate between the large ships on pitch black, moonless nights. Are you game?"

"I'm not a sailor."

"But you can speak several languages and fire a gun, can't you?"

"Give me a few days to think it over."

"Let me know by Saturday. There are a lot of yids willing to risk their lives to save the remaining Jews. And who knows, maybe Palestine will be a nation some day."

"Who's paying for all this, Nick?"

"I can't tell you. My uncle Tony knows, but he's not talking."

"Fair enough. I'll see you Saturday."

Jack had dropped in at Mama's after he had taken his son, William, to the Tot to Three School. He was stirring his coffee when Mama came into the kitchen.

"Heard from Mr. Brenner yet, Jacov?"

"Not yet. I'll call him later today."

She suddenly looked very old to him. Ida was wearing a faded housedress; and her once-streaked black hair had thinned and was now almost white, but she still kept it neatly tied in a bun resting on the nape of her neck. She sat down on a chair facing her son.

"Jacov, do you think we'll ever find Yehuda or his *kinder*?"

"I don't know. But Rubin and I will keep looking."

The sudden ring of the telephone excited them both. Mama got to it first. "Yes, Mr. Brenner, I know who you are. My son Jacov is here with me," and she handed the phone to Jack.

Mama noticed that Jack's face had turned pale.

"I'll tell her," he said into the phone, "but we'll keep on trying to trace Mosha."

"What has happened?" mama screamed.

"Vladimir is dead. He drowned trying to swim ashore from the shell of a broken Greek freighter that had burst into flames. The British kept shooting at the swimmers. He was not lucky. The Palmach have recovered his body."

Tears rolled down mama's cheeks. "Mosha—is my grandchild Mosha alive?"

"We don't know yet. Remember the Ascaro family, Mama?"

"The gengsters who lived on the first floor?"

"I met Nick, the one I went to school with, the other day. His uncle Tony is financing a fleet of small fishing boats from Greece and Italy and two from Marseilles that can bypass the British ships to rescue some of the survivors. The Jewish Agency has worked out some kind of deal with the British to let those who reach land stay, as long as they disappear from the coast. I've been offered a job to oversee the rescued survivors once they reach shore. *Kibbutzim* all over the country are waiting for those broken souls. Maybe Mosha is one of them."

"You can't go. I don't want to lose another son."

"I haven't said yes yet, Mama. The army trained me well, and I'm good with a gun and pretty tough with my fists."

"But you wanted to go back to college and maybe become a lawyer, my brilliant one."

"College will wait."

"And Bela?"

"She'll wait too."

Mama moved closer to Jack and wanted to hug him. Suddenly she grabbed hold of her chest with one hand and Jack's shirt with the other, tearing it off his shoulder. Then she slumped to the linoleum floor.

"Oy, Jacov, I'm dying …" And she closed her eyes.

Chapter 34

Rabbi Shneerson, the Lubivitcher Rebbe, was buried at Old Montefiore Cemetery in St. Albans, Queens, in a plot right in front of the Young Men's Brisker Society burial ground. His followers marched around his grave day and night, both guarding and watching, in case he miraculously rose from the earth to reign as the Messiah.

Mama was buried the day after she died in a plot behind the rabbi's at Old Montefiore Cemetery too. The iron gate with a lion of Judea engraved as a frontispiece was off its hinges and squeaked every time it was opened. But after a hundred years, it still looked impressive.

It was a simple graveside ritual alongside the resting places of a score of Russians and their families. Some had been Ida's friends and relatives in the old country who had also immigrated to the United States in the 1920s. Her sons had no illusions that she would rise from the dead but hoped that perhaps the famous *rebbe* in the neighboring plot would protect her.

Rabbi Feinstein recited the Psalm of David, ending with, "You shall dwell in the house of the Lord forever." Jack, Rubin, Louis, Nathan, and their wives and children sobbed softly as the simple wooden coffin was lowered into the ground. All four of Ida's sons recited the Kaddish, the mourner's prayer, and threw a handful of soil on top of the casket as was customary. The rabbi concluded his prayers with, "God has given, God has taken away, blessed be the name of God," and pinned a black ribbon with a cut corner on the left lapel of each son's jacket. As the family walked away, the diggers filled the grave with soil so no casket could be seen.

The brothers hugged each other, each one's tears landing on another's jacket lapels. The women cried somewhat louder, but Mama had reached her seventy-fifth birthday, and that was not exactly infancy. Jack spotted Nick Ascaro standing at the edge of the gathering. Before he could reach him, Nick drove off in a black Cadillac. The family returned to Rubin and Lota's house to sit shiva, the traditional seven-day mourning period for a Jewish family.

Guests came and went. They paid their condolences and shared a bagel, a hard-boiled egg, or a herring filet with the mourners. They praised the virtues of Ida, but Jack seemed inconsolable. He had not brought Mama's only wish from the battlefields of Europe home, her firstborn Yehuda, or at least one of his offspring. Where was Mosha? Vladimir, her protector and possible lover, was dead, but she was wandering somewhere, presumably alive and possibly lost.

At sundown on Friday, the shiva period recessed. Jack, unshaven and detached, threw on a windbreaker and walked down to the docks. He knew what he had to do, but first he had to talk with Rubin and Lota and finally convince Bela. That would not be easy.

Nick was waiting for him.

"Hi, friend … I'm so sorry. I remember your mother chasing me and my brothers with a broom when we played cops and robbers underneath her windows. I laugh about it now."

"Thanks for coming to the funeral, Nick. I saw you there. And your uncle Tony sent in a tray of kosher foods and a basket of rolls and bagels from Goldberg's Deli."

"In Italian families, eating softens the sorrow."

"In Jewish families, it doesn't take away the pain."

"I don't imagine you had time to think about Uncle Tony's offer. In two weeks, we leave for the Mediterranean, posing as the crew of a cargo ship. Tony has hired a group of small fishing boats from French, Greek, and Italian ports that can sail between the large British vessels and evade their big guns. Some of the guys were underwater scuba divers for the navy. They know how to save those washed overboard. We've got two dozen vets signed up already, and they're hot to trot. All of them are mad at the British. Those Palmach brigades helped them win the war in North Africa, and now they won't let them bring their blood brothers home."

"'Bela's not going to be happy about this."

"Bring her flowers and chocolates; make passionate love to her. If you're lucky, you'll knock her up and she'll love being pregnant. You're smart. Give us six months to help us get the Jew Fleet organized, and then I promise you'll go home. With what Tony's paying, we'll be swamped with volunteer replacements."

"Hey, Nick, what's making Tony so generous these days?"

"He's always had a warm spot for the Jews. He grew up among them. Besides, he has a Jewish wife he's still madly in love with."

"You guys were always chasing our women!"

"Ditto."

And the friends laughed.

"What about my son? He doesn't even recognize me as his father yet."

"What's his name?"

"William."

"I love kids and miss mine. My ex doesn't dare move out of New York."

Jack just listened and let Nick continue to try to persuade him to join the band of saviors.

"Don't worry. Ruby—I used to call him Ruby—and Lota will take good care of Bela and Little Willie. And who knows, with a stroke of luck we might even find Mosha among the refugees."

"I'll meet you again tomorrow, before the sun goes down. I have to continue sitting shiva, but I think I know what I have to do."

Jack walked back to the house of mourning.

Despite his sadness throughout the remaining days of shiva, Jack treated Bela with utter tenderness, patting her backside whenever she passed him, touching her whenever he sidled up to her at the kitchen counter. Especially at night, when his unshaven face brushed against hers, he covered her irritated skin with a myriad of kisses.

Before daylight came, visions of naked bodies piled alongside the crematoriums in the concentration camps he had seen and clothed bodies in makeshift bunks on flimsy fishing boats attempting to enter Palestine woke him. He grew miserable and restless. He tried to play with his son Willie, but at times he lost control, and the boy turned into Mosha, crumpled up in the corner of a deteriorating vessel, a skinny girl with a small belly protruding from her flimsy dress; Vladimir was not there. HIAS was probably right. He had likely been shot by a British soldier while swimming ashore.

One morning Bela woke early. There was Jack, packing his khaki duffel bag with underwear, a pair of dungarees, a few books, socks, a stack of T-shirts.

"Where are you going?" screeched Bela.

"Calm down, my love. I have to go abroad with the Jew Fleet, just for a few weeks."

"The Jew Fleet? Who are they?"

"A group of Jewish vets, and a few others, from all over the country and England who, like me, are determined to get the homeless Jews to Palestine. Nick has set up a meeting for tonight."

"And what about the business?"

"You and Ruby can handle the business. If Mosha is looking for us, I must find her."

"You're crazy! Your family in Brooklyn needs you. I need you. The presence of the Lubivitcher Rebbe's ghost near Mama's grave must have bewitched you. Spirits? Who would have believed that Lieutenant Sidowitz believed in spirits? Please, Jack, think it over. I love you."

"There's an old freighter being refitted in Williamsburg right now and 180 guys packing their duffel bags all over the country. We'll sail the *Brucha* to Lisbon, refuel and repair, and see what smaller boats Uncle Tony's contacts have assembled for us. The survivors, especially women and children, are waiting for us in detention camps along the coasts of Italy. The larger boats can't get through the British coastal blockade, but then we don't expect to land at Haifa."

"I know I can't persuade you not to go. Who knows if you'll ever find Mosha? HIAS might do a better job."

"But I have to try."

As a tear ran down her cheek, Bela managed to contain her surging emotions. "Close the door and come back inside our room. Can't you stay a few more nights?"

Chapter 35

everal days later, when the seven-day mourning period had ended, Bela awoke abruptly. Jack was not in the bed beside her. No lights were on in the house, and the khaki duffel bag he had been packing was gone. She could hear moving around in the room next door. Getting out of bed, she gazed out the window and saw that the old Chevy was still there. Nick Ascaro had probably picked Jack up. She was distressed. Her husband and lover hadn't even kissed her good-bye.

"Where are we headed, Nick?

"First we have to pick up some guns from Aunt Tess's bakery."

"You're kidding."

"No. Can you think of a better place to get them while you're buying fresh bread?"

"Only you Italians can think like that."

"Next we'll stop and see Uncle Tony at his club on Mulberry Street. And then? After an early dinner we'll head down to the Williamsburg docks. The bananas will have been unloaded. A crew is reloading the freighter with the supplies we're going to need. Food, clothing, medicines—all that kind of stuff."

"And the guns?"

"Yeah, we'll load those too."

"If fate smiles down on us, we might even need diapers."

Both men laughed.

"How many of us are sailing?"

"Forty on this first trip. We'll have plenty of time to plan strategies while crossing the Atlantic."

At the Madonna Café, the two men were ushered into the back room, where Uncle Tony hugged Jack. He remembered him from when their families had lived side by side in the old neighborhood.

"Welcome home, Lieutenant. You were always a smart boy. Sorry your mother died."

"So am I … I made her a promise I haven't been able to keep."

"Maybe you will yet. Nick told me all about it. I repeated your story to my friend Meyer Lansky in Miami. Mama Ida reminded him of his mother, and he almost cried. We've got all the money we need for this operation … and more. Here, come look at the details about the ship and fishing boats."

The tough-talking guy rolled out a massive schematic of the vessel and a detailed map of the coastlines of the Mediterranean. Every fishing village had been circled in red.

"Wow!"

"If this rescue mission succeeds, it'll ease my conscience. Since, as Nick told you, Terry, my wife, is Jewish, I promised to take her to the Promised Land, but first we have to help make a country. And I need Nick and another smart guy like you to help me do it. *Capesce?* Understand?"

After they studied the schematics and maps and shared information, it was suddenly late afternoon. Tony bellowed, "Antonio, we're hungry! It's time for a good veal Marsala and

Chianti or some other fine Italian wine from the cellar. Send Joey out for some fresh bread."

"Sure, boss. Give me a half hour."

By the time the Jack and Nick reached Pier Number 6, the autumn evening had cooled. A group of men were huddled around a banged-up oil drum with a fire going inside. A few were still rolling dollies of precut lumber up the gangplank. Someone had picked up a dozen cups of coffee from an all-night food cart; there was enough for Jack and Nick.

An anonymous crew member had painted over the name of the *Banana Manana* with blue maritime paint. Across the body of the ship in bold letters, it read BRUCHA. Except for Jack, no one seemed to know what it meant–blessing–and didn't seem to care. They all seemed eager to get aboard the boat, to set sail and finalize their plans. A huge map of the Mediterranean region had already been hung up on board, ready for them to study and highlight the small ports where fishing was the sustaining occupation.

"Do you think we might be taking the refugees to Atlit?"

"Atlit? Where's that? What's that?"

The one called the Professor took over. "It's a British concentration camp surrounded by barbed wire and twenty-four-hour sentries. Back in the '30s, anti-British Zionists were jailed there on the pretense of being traitors to the queen. Atlit is fifteen miles south of Haifa, but it might as well be fifteen hundred miles away. It is guarded by so many British soldiers that escape seems impossible."

"What are you saying–the British are holding these half-starved Jews captive?" Jack was angry.

"They give them enough to eat. Clean them up, delouse them, and make sure they aren't carrying any diseases. No one is tortured. When they accumulate several hundred Jews, they are shipped off to Mauritius, an island off the east coast of Africa."

"They might as well have stayed in the detention camps in Germany."

"What about the old and sick who survived?"

"The Haganah will get them down to Italy and out of Europe eventually, but they will have to wait. The men and women who made it to Palestine were the young and healthy ones, the ones who will build Israel.

"The British patrols, those sons of bitches, boarded and pulled them off their boats or out of the water if they had the courage to jump overboard. To please the Arabs and their oil interests, they won't let them leave the camp."

Nick's voice rose above the chatter of the men. "But at least they made it to Palestine temporarily. Getting them out of Atlit? That's Haganah's job."

"Where are we going?"

"To Lisbon," Nick announced. "There we'll refit the boat, paint it, and make it look like a cheap cruising vessel on holiday in the Mediterranean. We'll divide you guys into units and our supplies into usable packs. We'll dress like tourists, but stop at insignificant fishing villages that tourists usually don't go to and drop off men and supplies. The fishing boats are already there. One boat to one village. Tony has arranged all that with his compatriots in Palermo.

"Meanwhile, Haganah teams are roaming all over the boot. The Italians are lenient about letting out those who want to leave the detention camps and try to get to Palestine. Haganah finds them, collects them in groups of thirty or forty, and brings them by train or truck—or on foot—to a prearranged destination."

"Then where will we take them … fishing?"

"That's a secret for now."

Jack turned to Nick and quietly whispered, "Funny. Didn't see one security man on the dock tonight. No one even asked us what we were doing here or where we were going."

"You know my uncle Tony. Everyone on the dock owes him a favor."

The men finished their coffee, threw their empty cups into the oil drum, and watched them burn into embers. A big guy came out of nowhere carrying two pails of water. He doused the fire until there was not even one spark left. Then they all headed to the boat.

There were no lights, not even a full moon to witness the *Brucha's* departure.

On the first night at sea, Nick and Jack called a meeting in the galley, where a map had been hung on the long wall. The men peered with interest at an area of Europe and the Middle East that most had never seen before. A few, like Nick, had been part of the invasion of Italy and were a bit familiar with the many inlets that dotted the Mediterranean coastline. They measured the distances and mapped the routes from those inlets to Palestine. Their enthusiasm for the mission radiated throughout the boat.

"Fellas, pay attention!" Jack shouted. Using a long rubber-tipped pointer, he noted several inlets.

"In those towns, as of now, the fishing boats are waiting for us. The people there earn their living by fishing. We'll dress like fishermen and drink wine with them; those of you who can will speak their language. When the fish are unloaded at the end of the day, about thirty survivors and ten of us, dressed like the Italians, will board the boat and take off for Palestine. There, when darkness falls we shall sneak between the British destroyers and go north until we reach Ceasarea or Shefayim. The displaced thirty will be dropped on the shore, where Haganah scouts will be waiting to escort them to Kibbutz Sharon up in the Carmel Mountains. They are expected."

"So what happens to us?"

"We take the fishing boat back to the Italian town, go aboard the *Brucha*, and sail to the next village, where the next group of survivors will be waiting."

Every day, the crew gathered in the galley and reviewed the plans. They built bunks for sleeping, updated the kitchen, and prepared the old tramp freighter to accommodate men, women, and children instead of fruit. They divided themselves into units and made lists for the clothes, nets, and fishing equipment they would have to buy in Lisbon.

Jack was amazed how much Nick had learned about navigation and sailing. For his Italian friend, this was an adventure; for Jack, it was a spiritual calling.

"Why Portugal, Nick?"

"Italy is too far away. We need to refuel and make sure the *Brucha* is in good shape. Eventually we'll need the ship to come back to America. And Portugal has remained a neutral country before, during, and after the war. Its major port, Lisbon, is a beautiful city with Moorish architecture, sidewalk cafés, and refugees of every nation, all seeking a way to get to the United States or South America. French, Portuguese, Spanish, and Italian, plus African dialects, can be heard on the streets."

"How do you know all this?"

"Your friend Nick gets around. I once had a Portuguese girlfriend."

No one paid attention to the *Brucha* as it moored at a maritime repair shop; the sailors, unshaven, dressed in coarse dark trousers and fisherman-knit sweaters, some sporting berets, descended on the city.

"Back at eight tonight, guys," Nick bellowed in Italian.

"Hey, Bruno, you're the cook. See if you can get some fresh fish we can fry for dinner. All the boats are coming in with their day's catch."

"Aren't you two coming with us?"

"No. We've got to finalize some things in town with some of Tony's *paisans*. The envelopes that will seal the deal were delivered to me a few minutes ago. Mike, you and Larry stay aboard and keep an eye on things."

"Sure, Nick."

The crew members each went their own ways. They mingled with the people on the streets, including Germans, who had removed their military uniforms but looked at the rest of them as if they still owned Europe even though they had lost the war. The cafés were crowded with fishermen, diplomats, and spies who were relishing creamy Portuguese pastries and afternoon drinks.

Bruno bought fresh tilapia from a boat that had just docked and long loaves of fresh bread from a bakery in an alley between two medieval buildings. Further down the alley were shops with piles of rubber boots and waterproof jackets, scaling knives and maritime scissors. Since Spain and Portugal both shared the Iberian Peninsula, many of the shopkeepers also spoke Spanish. Juan Arnez, a seaman from Puerto Rico, enjoyed bargaining with the vendors before purchasing additional clothes and sweaters to keep any of the refugees they might rescue warm.

They stopped for drinks at the dockside *ginja* bar and socialized with sailors and other patrons from many nations; most were drinking a Portuguese liqueur made from berries. They listened to the conversations between the other drinkers. It seemed as if everyone was spying on everyone else. They wanted to share any suspicious information with Jack and Nick.

When they got back to the *Brucha*, they could smell potatoes frying. Bruno brought the fresh fish into the galley kitchen. Dinner would be ready soon. The men were not only hungry but eager to find out why Nick and Jack had gone off by themselves.

Chapter 36

Contrary to what Jack and Nick had expected, the reticent crew at the table remained stone-faced, except for an occasional, harsh yelp from a hungry seaman.

"Pass the ketchup, you at the end."

"Hey, where's the bread?"

"Juan, the fish is good. Any seconds?"

No one looked Jack or Nick squarely in the face, but each man knew what the others wanted to ask.

Finally the Professor broke the quiet. "Thanks for not sharing. When were you going to let us know what's going on? We'll be more open. We picked up a lot of street knowledge at the bar while you were working out strategies in some fancy hotel, I bet. These are the rumors.

"The liberated Jews are penniless and have nowhere to go except south. No nation wants them or is willing to return their property.

"A few have tried digging up buried treasure, but somebody always got there first.

"The British are determined to keep them out of Palestine lest they offend the oil-rich Arab states.

"And ... where the hell are the fishing boats?"

Jack finally joined the conversation. "Each is in a harbor in a fishing village. They are low-silhouette boats, so close to the waterline that they will be very hard to see from the decks of the British destroyers."

"Has it been done before?"

"One Greek boat and one from Romania, our sources tell us, succeeded last month. But they only transported a limited number of refugees. The boats were so old and leaky that the passengers have to know how to swim.

"Okay, guys, relax. Here's what we found out today from Tony's contact in Lisbon. The fishing boats have already been delivered to ten small fishing villages along the Italian coast, starting from Catania just near Palermo. A Portuguese captain who knows how to navigate the Straits of Gibraltar and the Mediterranean will arrive here tomorrow morning. Pay close attention to everything he has to show you. If we're lucky, he'll speak Portuguese, Italian, and some English. He's no kid and has been fishing in these waters since before the war. He also knows at least one or more seamen in each of the designated fishing villages. Listen carefully to what he says and watch him sail this old tub. He has assured us that it's seaworthy.

"In the next day or two, you'll decorate the boat with flags and banners we picked up from a dealer far from the marketplace so no one would notice. We'll make the *Brucha* look like a low-cost cruise ship hosting a plumber's convention. We'll play lively music, watch some movies we brought along, talk loud, drink moderately, and say nothing of value."

"How about getting through the Straits of Gibraltar?"

Nick took over. "The captain knows everybody at the Rock, so there will be no problem getting through the straits, especially when the customs inspectors share a good bottle of

Spanish brandy. After we reach the Mediterranean, we'll sail on to Palermo. Tony's compadres will be waiting for us."

"Can they be trusted?" a Jew-boy turned sailor asked.

"They'll follow orders or face the consequences. The toughest guys in Sicily are Uncle Tony's first cousins, and they are grateful that the Allies liberated their island."

"Are you sure?" a second sailor chimed in.

"Enough green has been passed around. We'll refuel, pick up provisions and other supplies, and see what news has filtered south from northern Italy," said Nick.

Jack stood up and took control of the conversation. "Maybe after that we'll be able to let you know where our first stop for the rescue mission begins and who of us takes the first shift."

As Nick and Jack walked away, Jack whispered, "The Palmach have their own contacts. I hope we'll be ready to work together."

Jack had been so busy preparing the vessel for its voyage that he'd forgotten to write to Bela. He knew that she and the others at home would be worried about him. And he owed his wife an apology.

At four in the morning. he put on a pea jacket, picked up a pen and paper, tucked his cigarettes and Zippo lighter into his pocket, and went upstairs. A dim light from the dock made it possible to barely see what he was writing, and he settled into a corner of the ship. A few African émigrés were cleaning the piers below.

Dear Bela:

I'm sitting on an old freighter waiting to start our journey. I'm excited, and so are the other vets who have volunteered for this mission. Here in Lisbon, with Uncle Tony's money, we have found everything we need for us and the survivors we hope to save. From here, I can see the outline of the lovely city, but none of it, or its women, is as beautiful as you. When this mission ends, whether I find Mosha or not, I promise to love you forever, not only in bed. We have so much to be thankful for.

Say hello to the family.

Love again,

Jack

Jack folded the aerogram with its writing inside and walked over to the ship's rails.

"Abak," he called.

"Is it you, Lieutenant Jack?"

"Yes. I'll pay you double the postage and a tip if you mail this letter for me first thing tomorrow morning. I'll be gone by then, but I'll be coming back."

"I trust you, Lieutenant Jack. If letter for girlfriend–or wife–I do it."

Jack ran down the gangplank and handed the letter to Abak. "Don't disappoint me, Abak."

"Never, Lieutenant."

As Jack returned to the *Brucha,* he was blocked by a big man with his arms spread out, drinking from a small glass. It was Sebastian Hector de Milo, a weathered veteran of the waters alongside Portugal, striding up the gangplank of the freighter as if he owned it. He poked a crewman, who was napping at the entrance to the ship.

"Get up," he ordered. "I'm here to teach you how to sail this tub, and you're all sleeping! From now on, address me as Captain de Milo."

"I'm Lieutenant Jack Sidowitz, the co-leader of this crew. I assume you are the Portuguese navigator."

"Sorry, Lieutenant, I didn't see you. Tell this sleepy bastard to get all the crew up on deck. We haven't got all day. I want to shove off before the sun rises."

"Yes, sir," Juan, who was usually the cook, responded, and fled down to the crewmen's bunks.

In seconds, half-dressed, some carrying their socks and sneakers, the men gathered around Captain de Milo, as they had been told he preferred to be called.

"Ready, guys?" he yelled. "We sail before sunrise. Not too many boats will be out there. Which one of you knows anything about maritime engines?"

The Jew-boy from the Bronx timidly raised his hand, to the astonishment of his fellow crewmates. "My father owns the City Island Mariner Club, and I've been running outboard and inboard motors since I was seven. And I was a seaman first class in the US Navy until two months ago, assigned to the engine room of a supply ship crossing the Atlantic."

"Engines on freighters are a little different, but come with me," Captain de Milo said in perfect English. "The rest of you will be assigned to various tasks by Nick. Jack, keep an eye on navigation instruments and the maps for the course we need to follow once we go through the Straits of Gibraltar."

Before long, the men, busy with chores, could feel the boat leaving the harbor. Most had forgotten about breakfast and had already gotten their sea legs. Captain de Milo was heard instructing the Jew-boy, who seemed to be doing everything right. It would take a day and a half to get to Gibraltar, the peninsula that separated Europe from Africa. Still a British colony, the town sat on its high point; the Rock of Gibraltar and its port emptied into the Mediterranean. Its official language was

English, but because of its proximity to the Iberian Peninsula, many businessmen spoke Spanish and Portuguese as well.

The crew took turns eating and sleeping. All day and night, many ships passed through the straits in both directions. No one appeared to have noticed the *Brucha*. And there were no toll collectors.

Sebastian knew all the traffic rules for sailing through the Straits, and the freighter entered the southern lane, where the easterly currents increased the speed of the passage. Sebastian had Abie slow the freighter as the ship neared the Gibraltar Administration Station, and he waved to the group of men on its observation deck. They seemed to know him and waved back. Without stopping at dockside, he handed a package to the pilot of a tugboat that came close enough to the boat, and Abie, the Jew-boy who had finally gotten a name, could hear him say "Thank you" to Sebastian.

It was sunny, fifty-eight degrees and beautiful, as the boat entered the Mediterranean and headed for the boot of Italy.

Chapter 37

I t was surprisingly cold on deck, and the seamen were glad they had bought heavy sweaters and gloves in Lisbon. The sea was blue, calm, and beautiful, and they could imagine sailing it for pleasure in the spring.

The small city of Catania stuck out into the Mediterranean. A day later they sailed to a pier at the end of the harbor. The street adjacent to the docks was awash with vendors, shoppers, and ladies of the night who were walking the streets looking for matinee business or evening appointments. Mixed in with what looked like local inhabitants were emaciated pairs of men and women with sunken eyes that seemed to dart out of their sockets. They ignored the glances of some of the pedestrians and with an air of chutzpah drifted to the end of the pier where the *Brucha* was docked.

An empty oversized fishing vessel had pulled along aside the freighter. It smelled of the sea.

Captain de Milo called to them in Portuguese. "Two of you, topside now! Let the others get the boat ready to go. Load the ones who look the youngest and the hungriest, and give them something to eat. If they look too well fed, tell them to wait for the next trip."

The men on the fishing boat laughed.

Then he turned back to Jack and listened as the lieutenant gave orders to the entire crew.

"Guys, the first fishing boat is here. Fresh water is being put on board. We'll need a crew of seven. Who wants to take the first trip?"

All of the hands shot up.

"Some of you will have to wait. Nick, assisted by Captain de Milo, will be in charge. Juan, take care of provisions and meals. Nothing too spicy; their stomachs aren't ready. Professor, you'll be Nick's navigator. Keep studying the charts, and keep us pointed in the right direction as Milo checks the engines. The Palmach guys will guide you. They know these waters thoroughly."

He tapped a few other guys on their shoulders. "You'll round out the crew."

Those who had not been chosen looked downcast.

"Don't pout, the rest of you. I'll take the second boat from another port in Italy. You'll be coming with me or waiting for the third trip. Let's see how the first two turn out.

"By the way, on every trip, some of the Palmach who rounded up the survivors will be sailing with you for protection. They know where the final destination is and have enough weapons to make sure nothing stops you from getting there."

Sebastian de Milo added, "We'll make it fine."

"I have one more thing to say," Jack said. "If any of you comes across a girl named Mosha, maybe pregnant, let Nick know. She's of special interest to me."

The sailors looked at each other. Some winked rather salaciously. They knew Jack, but only Nick knew about Vladimir.

As the crew taking the first run got ready to descend the

ladder of the freighter, they saw two men loading their human cargo into the fishing boat.

"The *Brucha*" Jack continued, "will be waiting there with a fresh fishing boat. Your boat will return to the port of Lecce, minus the survivors, for maintenance. We'll meet you there; provided your boat avoids the British destroyers and took our human cargo safely to Palestine. After a few hours of R&R together, and after we've shared all the details we need to know, our second group will be ready to go. There's a wide-open DP camp north of the town on the Ionian Sea. The Palmach is organizing it now."

"Good luck and God bless you all!" the Portuguese captain concluded as he drank from the mysterious vial that he kept hidden in his jacket.

Chapter 38

The crew named the fishing boat *Aleph*. She and the freighter left Catania at the same time. They both headed south into the Ionian Sea. The *Brucha* sailed around the heel of the Italian boot into the historic city of Lecce. From the upper deck, the crew could see the tops of the baroque cathedrals that had been famous throughout Europe for two thousand years. A smaller ship on their port side was loading Lecca stone for export to a sculptors' commune in Florence. Crates with bottles from the wineries outside the city limits were relegated to starboard.

Jack had never seen such concentrated beauty during his days in Germany. He wondered how the Italians had escaped the mass destruction of their country's heritage, for they had been Hitler's ally for part of the war. The country was ultimately rescued by American and British soldiers and airmen with careful instructions to avoid damaging the great sculpture and architecture the Italians were noted for.

The fishing boat headed due east into the Mediterranean, not far from the coast of Africa, toward Palestine.

It would be a long wait before they could all come together and find out if their mission had been successful.

Many days had passed before Abie, who was on watch up in the crow's nest, yelled out, "Everyone, out and topside!" Adjusting his binoculars, he looked out to sea. "A small boat is heading this way. It seems to be coming into port. I think there are only a few men on it."

"Are there seven?" Jack yelled back.

"I don't know for sure, Lieutenant."

The rest of the crew arrived on deck as the fishing boat smoothly slipped into the berth next to the *Brucha*. Two sailors secured the smaller boat to the freighter, and then all seven from the fishing boat came aboard. Jack hugged Nick and then shook hands with the rest of the men.

He smiled at their bearded faces. "I think you all need a shave before we sit down to talk."

"How about a shower and some beer?"

"Okay, okay. Thank God all seven of you are safe!" Striving to contain his anxiousness, Jack managed to inquire, "And the survivors?"

"Ashore in Palestine. They had to walk through water for the final distance, but it was shallow. And we got them past the British ships unseen. No one panicked. There were twenty-four men, twelve women, and four children. The mothers nursed the two infants so they wouldn't cry as they were carried to land."

"Wow."

"The fishing boat was so low that it hardly reached above the water line, and it was as dark as the moonless sea. We were lucky. No wonder they call them low-silhouette boats. The rest is up to the Palmach. It's their job to get them safely to a designated kibbutz.

"Suddenly we heard gunfire. We never left the boat but turned around and headed back here."

"Anything else to tell me, friend?"

"No. Nobody'd heard of Mosha. I asked a few refugees on the boat. The name Vladimir didn't ring a bell either. We'll share the details after the men and I get cleaned up."

"Sorry to interrupt," said Juan. "One of the Palmach who spoke Spanish told me a story of a young, tough survivor called Vladimir who jumped overboard on a previous trip, intending to swim ashore. He hit his head on a corner of a British ship and disappeared. We believed that his body floated to the beach. It was assumed he was dead. The next morning his body was gone. No one knows who might have picked it up, dead or alive."

Jack wondered if he would have more luck on the next trip out. He knew he might need help from God.

Chapter 39

The crew named the second fishing boat *Bet*, the next boat destined for the dangerous mission to bring stranded survivors to the shores of Palestine. They had learned a lot from the returning sailors, who had picked up the first survivors in Lecce; the mission had succeeded.

Sitting around the galley kitchen as Juan, the cook, served dinner, the *Bet* crew posed endless questions before departure time.

"Was the voyage safe?"

"Yeah, no rough seas. The Mediterranean is a piece of cake. No foreign ships coming alongside and asking questions."

"What were the survivors like?" asked Jack.

"Mostly young, angry, and ready to fight when they got to Palestine. Some were talkative; others silent."

Nick picked up the discussion. "We heard tales of murder, mutilation, beatings, and rapes, plus criticism of the American occupiers in Germany for not releasing survivors is spreading throughout Europe."

"I must write Bela and my brothers about what you are telling me."

"A lot of you Americans won't believe this for a long time. History will have to tell the true story," asserted the Professor.

"Some of the survivors risked their lives to escape from American DP camps that they said were as bad as the German ones had been, except there were no ovens. Some blamed General Eisenhower and General Patton for not caring."

But some of the crew was only interested in the excitement and compensation of the voyage.

Milo interjected, "How long did it take?"

"Twelve hours. I thought it would have been longer."

"Were seven of you enough?"

"I think so. We didn't get in each other's way, and the Palmach contributed two extra hands when they were needed."

"Where did you land?"

"We didn't actually land."

"What do you mean?" queried Abie.

"We sailed north of the British blockade. Near Haifa we reached a narrow opening between two gigantic warships. Milo's charts showed us the depth of the water near the shores of Palestine. We knew how far we could sail toward shore in the darkness, and the Palmach had prepared our passengers to walk the remaining distance. They all wore dark clothes. No babies allowed; no children under four feet tall."

Jack jotted down a lot of the comments and turned to Nick. "Nick, you're in charge of the freighter now. Keep it in good shape. Before you leave port, find out if there is an American Consul in town and get friendly with its employees."

The crew members went their own way; some rested, others played cards. Jack wrote another letter to Bela.

Dearest Bela,

Just want to remind you how much I love you and how lucky we are to be Americans.

The first leg of our mission has been successful. Every man, woman, or child we rescue is one more step in the future of the Jewish people and the possibility of having a country of our own.

I'll share the details when we get home. Just a few more months, I hope.

By the way, I've grown a beard ... not a long one. Promise I'll shave it off before we make love, unless you like to be tickled. Anything you want!

Kiss Willie, Lota, and my brothers for me.

Your faithful husband,
Jack

"I've changed our plans a little," said Jack a few hours later. "We're all sailing to Crete together. *Alpha* will be left behind here, and a second fishing boat will be waiting for us. Milo has a Greek uncle there who works undercover with Irgun, a tough group of Palestinian ex-British soldiers interested in recruiting potential fighters to their cause. The Greek rescuers brought a group of Jews to Crete by ferry from Italy and are hiding them until we get there. They'll load the forty of them on the fishing boat, and we'll take over. Nick and most of you will remain on the freighter and make any necessary repairs until we return."

"Why are the Greeks helping us?" Abie asked.

"The Jews and the Greeks on the island have always been friendly. But when the Germans overran the island, they killed almost all of the two hundred Jews who lived there and destroyed Heraklion. The Cretan locals resisted fiercely; the Germans retaliated, and with the help of the British the enemy was defeated. But the Greeks are not too fond of the British for lots of other reasons."

"I know Crete is closer to Israel, but why the change?" the Professor asked.

"Another reason to throw the British off guard. Also, we've been sailing too close to the shores of North Africa. There was nearly a collision outside of Tunis on our first run. Tunis, I've heard, is often known to pirate ships."

"I'll make some changes on the charts," Milo offered. "Abie, do you hear me?"

"Yes, sir. Is the cargo being loaded?"

"It's not dark enough."

"By the way, Milo, locate Shefalim on the charts. Find the depth of its harbor. It's eighteen miles north of Haifa. That might be where we are going," Jack said.

Two days later was an encore of the night the *Alpha* had left Lecce, but tonight was the *Bet*'s turn. Jack had posted his second v-mail to Bela from Heraklion. In the darkness at four thirty that morning, pairs of ill-clad, anemic couples appeared at the boat. All carried small packages that probably would not reach shore if they had to walk far through the water. But they gave them comfort.

Jack watched from the deck as they were helped into the smaller boat moored next to the *Brucha*. He counted thirty-nine. Then he and his crew transferred to the fishing boat.

With the help of a seaman, a small-framed straggler was the last to step into the boat from the mooring, wrapped in a long coat and an extra shawl for warmth. At first Jack could not tell if it was a man or woman. The walk was daintier than a man's, the hands long and fingers slim as she tightened the shawl around her. The passenger took the last remaining seat at the stern of the boat and muttered what sounded like a prayer.

Jack could not take his eyes off the straggler. Something

about her walk and the way she held her head reminded him of someone he'd known before.

"Ahoy," called Nick from the deck of the freighter. "While we're gone, friend, check and see if there is an American Consul in Heraklion."

"I already did it in Lecce."

"Do it again. I might need their services here instead. Just do it."

Suddenly, from the direction of Heraklion, police sirens wailed, and the lights of two cars pointed right at the freighter, illuminating the darkness. The whole operation was illegal, and perhaps someone had squealed.

Jack waved to the men on the freighter and cast off, and the *Bet* departed the harbor, heading straight for the center of the Mediterranean. A small two-man sailboat sporting a blue flag with a crescent began tailing it. Jack revved up the engine and outran the day sailer.

Jack thought about Mosha as he steered the vessel towards Palestine and tried to picture what she had looked like back in the displaced persons camp. She had been a meek and skinny girl. If the straggler was Mosha, she might still be meek and skinny. He waited for a pause in his duties to approach her.

Before he could do so, the Mediterranean turned turbulent, and the straggler and other passengers became seasick and retched into the choppy blue waters. It was a few hours before the sea grew calm; the passengers slept where they sat, tired and scared of what was coming.

Before daylight, Jack saw the mysterious woman stir. He tapped her on the shoulder and gently said, "Mosha? Are you Mosha Vinkovsky?

She stared up into his face. "Lieutenant Sidowitz?"

"Yes, the American officer from Brest-Litovsk. Your uncle.

I haven't forgotten how to speak Russian. I hoped I would, but I didn't expect to find you. You know we're on our way to Palestine to save many of you from being detained in Europe."

"I've tried before, but I lost Vladimir!" Tears rolled down her face.

"When?"

"About two months ago. These men with a strange language—sort of like the language I heard in the synagogue—came to the camp, crowded us onto buses and then onto ferries that took us to Crete. We were packed into every inch of a big Italian cruiser, the *Leonardo da Vinci*, expecting to get to Palestine. As we got closer to shore, the British stopped us and turned their big guns on us. The *Leonardo* was not equipped to respond. We were forced to turn back to Europe. Vladimir, rather than return to a camp again, jumped overboard and tried to swim ashore. I don't know how to swim, so I was returned to the displacement camp in Italy.

"The others said he probably died, but I won't believe them. Vladimir's father was a swimming coach in Russia, and he learned how to swim as a child. I know he was a powerful swimmer and a survivor."

"We'll try to find out. If not, I'll take you back to Crete with me and possibly get you back to America. We're blood relatives, and I'm a veteran. That gets me special privileges with the US Consul."

"I can't go back without him. I have to find Vladimir, or at least try."

"Everyone in America is waiting. You are the only hope that a part of our oldest brother is alive. You'll have a good home there; we'll get you a job while you go to night school."

"In Brest, I was studying to be a nurse."

"You still can. Your uncles in Brooklyn can make it possible. You also have lots of cousins, teenage ones and little ones."

"But they are not my beloved."

Jack was surprised at her last word, but he understood that she would not come with him until they had exhausted every possibility to discover whether Vladimir might still be alive.

"But my sweet Mosha, first we have to get you to Palestine."

Chapter 40

In the quiet of the night, the *Bet* made its way to Palestine. A quarter moon, occasionally obscured by a cloud, created inky darkness, and followed the boat with its sleeping refugees.

The Palmach officer strode over to Jack and introduced himself. "Shalom, I'm Ari Ben Adami. What may I call you, sir?"

"On this voyage, just plain Jack will be fine. I used to be Lieutenant Sidowitz in the army, but I was Jacov before I went to America."

Ari smiled. "My grandfather's name was Jacov before he came to Palestine, and it still is. It's a good name for a good person. Did you serve in Europe?"

"Yes, Ari, I was an interpreter for the US Army. The war in Europe had just ended. Masses of crippled and sick survivors poured out of what we now call concentration camps. Am I speaking too quickly for you?"

"No, Jacov … Sorry, Jack. I learned English at school at the same time that I spoke Hebrew at home."

Jack grew animated and his speech accelerated, "The survivors were running helter-skelter, here, there, and everywhere, but they had no place to go. So many were dead; so many were dying."

"Did they all look like skeletons, Jack?"

"They were all hungry ... The Germans had tried to starve them."

Ari had many more questions. He was only twenty years old and had never before met an American soldier. "So where did you find Mosha?"

"It's a long story."

"It's a long night," said the younger man.

"Okay, you win. I had promised our mother that I would try to find Yehuda, her eldest son, the one who had not come to America with us. Since the Allies had spontaneously opened the camps, there was no time for implementing rules of departure. Refugees from everywhere were aimlessly traveling the Continent. My commanding officer, who is also a Jew, gave me a three-day pass to look for my brother or any of his family who might have survived the brutality of the Germans.

"Earlier I had stopped at a forced labor camp where a young, angry boy who had been liberated by the Americans latched on to me in order to get scraps to eat. His name was Vladimir, and he had been in three labor camps previously. He knew his way in and out, under fences, and into bunks. It was easy for him to talk with the other unfortunates and get them to share their heartache.

"He came from a city near Brest-Litovsk and, coincidently, had gone to *khayder* with a boy named Vinkovsky, an uncommon Russian name. He mingled with the young people and met a young girl named Mosha. Her surname was also Vinkovsky. It was her brother who had gone to Hebrew school with Vladimir. My tagalong introduced her to me. After a few pleasantries and a chocolate bar I had in my pocket, she stopped being awed by my uniform. We began sharing our families' histories. There was no doubt in my mind that Mosha was my brother Yehuda's granddaughter."

"Couldn't you get her out of Germany through the American Consul in Berlin?" Ari asked.

"I might have, but before I could even get an appointment, Romeo and Juliet decided they wanted to go to Israel and ran off to a camp in Italy where the Palmach was recruiting."

The Palmachi and Israeli-to-be rested his chin in his hands and sat in thought for a moment. "Vladimir … did you say his name was Vladimir?"

Jack nodded.

"I met a Vladimir with Mosha on the *Leonardo da Vinci,* the passenger ship that tried to get over a thousand men, women, and children to Palestine, but it was blocked by the British and returned to Europe. Vladimir and a few others jumped overboard. It was assumed that they were either shot by the British or had drowned."

"So I've heard," acknowledged Jack.

Ari continued. "But the next morning, Schlomo, a fisherman near Caesarea, found a boy stretched out on the sand. He was hardly breathing, but he was alive. He wore a few rags where clothes had once been, but no identification papers were in his shredded back pocket. The numbers the Germans had tattooed on his arm would eternally be there."

Jack gasped.

"With flags, Schlomo signaled another fisherman who was bringing in his boat. He came ashore, and together they picked up the boy and loaded him into the day's catch. The faint odor of fresh fish covered the scent of a dying body as they rowed north to a cove. The boy's breathing remained shallow but steady. From there they carried him to a nearby hospital."

"Was it Vladimir?" Jack asked.

"I don't know yet. We've forwarded the numbers on his arm to Tel Aviv. Our office is tracking them now."

"Have you told Mosha? She has to know," implored Jack.

"I will as soon as I am sure. I don't want her disappointed. I think she may be pregnant like my wife," Ari said, "she's throwing up a lot. Thank goodness, it's over the side of the boat. They were so in love that if Vladimir is alive she won't leave him."

"Miracle of miracles. Yehuda might have had a great-grandchild. Ari, let's get some sleep," said Jack. "I'm so glad we had this talk. There'll be lots to find out and lots to do tomorrow."

Before morning dawned, when it was still dark, the *Bet* approached Palestine, glided on to a sandbar, and dropped anchor fifty feet from the beach. Jack approached Mosha again.

"We disembark in ten minutes. There's still time to change your mind. Come back with me to Crete. Nick's uncle's friends control the ships coming in and out of the island and will help get you to America. We'll worry about the legality once we're there. The family is waiting."

"I can't, Uncle Jacov. May I call you uncle?"

"I am your uncle."

"I love you, but I love Vladimir differently. Ours is a man-and-wife kind of love."

Without comment, Jack accepted her answer.

"Can you walk through the water once you get off the sandbar? It can be deeper than you think."

"I'd go through fire and ice to find him."

"Even in your condition?"

"Condition?" Mosha seemed surprised.

"You're expecting a baby, aren't you?"

"How did you know?"

"Ari suspected."

"Ssh," Ari cautioned. "See the shadows on the land? They are Palmach soldiers, men and women who will guide you off the boat and to the trails up into the woods. At the top of the hill, you'll be in Kibbutz Shefayim. The fields are full of cotton now and ready for picking. Once you are settled, you'll be just another kibbutznik growing vegetables, feeding animals, and primarily getting cotton, their cash crop, ready for market."

Ari added, "Don't worry, Mosha, there's a doctor and a midwife at the kibbutz. You'll be safe."

Mosha turned to Jack and put her arms around him. "Don't worry, I'll find Vladimir. I have your address and will let you know where we are and how to reach us."

"Do that as soon as you can. I'll start the immigration process with HIAS. Remember you're related to a veteran. That will help. Now I have to get back to Crete."

Mosha turned back to Jack and put her arms around him. "Don't worry, I'll find Vladimir. We'll all be together someday soon."

Jack felt assured by the confidence and maturity the girl had developed in such a short time. He hugged her one more time before Ari carried her off the fishing boat and onto dry land. Then he watched her struggle up the hill to search for Vladimir.

Chapter 41

Back in Crete, Jack realized it was time for him to return to America. He had heard from one of his crew that veterans were having a tough time getting jobs, and more American, Canadian, and other recruits were attracted to *Brucha* and ready to expand the Jewish Fleet. Jack and Nick's venture had been a noble beginning.

Abie had matured into an excellent captain, and most of the new arrivals had served in the navy during WWII. Jack was sure that more displaced persons would get to the Promised Land.

And he couldn't stop dreaming about Bela.

From Crete, he managed to get a fisherman to take him to Lisbon, where Tony, Nick's uncle, had already prepared papers for him and listed him as a crewman on the manifest of one of his cargo ships that was carrying Portuguese pottery to New York. Jack was friendly enough with the seamen he worked alongside, but he never told them that he was Lieutenant Jack Sidowitz, veteran of the US Army.

Days later, at a pier in Brooklyn, they unloaded the ship. Jack said his good-byes and hurried home. No one answered the doorbell. He was disappointed, but he knew Bela would come back. So he sat on the stoop and waited, picturing Little Willie jumping from one box to another on the hopscotch board the children had chalked on the sidewalk.

To pass the time, he started searching his jacket pockets. Stuffed in the back, still damp, he found an unopened letter from Bela that he had forgotten to read in his haste to board the cargo ship.

Darling,

It's been so long since I heard from you, but I love you more than ever. The last night we loved each other, God was kind to us. We are expecting another child in several months. Hope you are here for his or her birth.

Please, my Jack, come home. I read about the refugees you have smuggled into Palestine, but there is much to do here to convince our country to recognize Israel as a nation. President Truman had a Jewish friend and business partner and is not as anti-Semitic as so many of the other senators. The Daily Forward *says that Truman is inclined to vote yes, when and if the UN Assembly considers statehood for Israel ... but who knows.*

The rest of the family and business is good.
Love and kisses,
Bela

Jack read the letter over and over again, until he saw a little boy walking down the street holding his mother's hand. The mother's rounded belly led the way. Jack stood on the sidewalk and opened his arms wide. There was no way Bela and Willie could avoid walking into his welcome.

Months went by. There were dinners and parties and

business to attend to. The baby was born at the end of the year, a rosy, seven-pound little girl with wavy black hair like her father Jack's.

In the synagogue, they named her Idalynn in honor of her grandmothers, and all the brothers and their families were there to celebrate. Jack went to see Mrs. Stein at HIAS and filled out all the papers that were relevant to bringing Mosha to America. No one yet knew if Vladimir was alive. Nor had they heard if Mosha had given birth.

The family talked about it but could do nothing but wait. Displaced persons continued to be smuggled into Palestine as she prepared to become the State of Israel, with or without UN permission. They contributed to HIAS and the Jewish National Fund, leaders in the fight for an independent Jewish nation.

Jack loved his dinners at home with his family, playing with the children, and making love to his adoring wife. But he wanted more.

"Bela, darling, do you think you can take care of the children without my help? I want to register for college this fall."

"College? We have two children now. Aren't you happy in the business with Ruby? We make a good living."

"I know, but I want to turn it into a corporation, not a mom-and-pop shop. I want to expand our product line and include bags, wallets, and maybe shoes. I want to turn Belabelts into a leader in New York's garment center and abroad. I may be a good salesman, but for that I need education. I'm not even sure what economics really means."

"Can we afford it?"

"The GI Bill will pay for my schooling. That's one benefit of being a veteran. And I'd attend classes at night and weekends. As I learn, I'll run the business side of Belabelts even better. I don't trust outsiders."

Bela walked up to Jack, put her arms around him, and lifted her face to his.

"I love you enough to let you do whatever makes you happy. I always knew you would succeed, from the first time you managed to get into the locked building on West Thirty-Seventh Street when we first met. Willie is almost ready for school. I'll design at home again and hire a nanny for Idalynn if I have to. But we will build this business empire together."

"What about Lota and Ruby?"

"Oh, Jack, they'll agree. Just let Ruby run the factory and deal with the workers. Equal partners, each of you running the part of the business you know best."

"Bela, you're not only smart; you're beautiful."

And he took her hand and led her into the bedroom.

Chapter 42

The economy of the country was booming. Every vet wanted a car; his wife wanted a ranch house in suburbia; and a plentitude of babies were conceived and born across the country.

By 1947, the Sidowitz family was prospering. Jack gave all his efforts to the business, and Bela designed and patented a smashing tote handbag large enough to hold everything, including extra diapers. Jack hired vets as traveling salesmen for Belabelts, and the fashion line was reviewed in *Women's Wear Daily.* The department stores in Chicago, Miami, and Washington, DC, liked what they saw and Bela's designs were featured in <u>Mommy and Baby Magazine</u> throughout the country.

Jack and Bela bought an older brick house in a fashionable, tree-lined neighborhood two blocks away from Rubin and Lota and in walking distance of Brooklyn College. Jack registered for night classes at BC for the spring semester.

He wrote to Mosha several times at the kibbutz address she had given him, but he never received a reply. He had no idea if Vladimir was alive, whether Mosha had given birth to a healthy baby, or where they were.

The family followed with growing disillusionment the

news coming out of the Middle East and America's lack of enthusiasm about declaring an Israeli state.

On Saturdays, Jack often studied. After a few hours, he'd grow restless and go out to see if the mail had been delivered. To his surprise, a few foreign stamps occupied the corner of a thin envelope. With trembling hands, he opened the envelope. Two sheets of paper were covered in Russian writing, and he saw a photograph. The caption on the photograph of a man and woman and a little boy, no more than eighteen months old read, "Mosha, Vladimir, and Yehuda Isiah Solikov." He leaned against the mailbox and read aloud. He didn't care if all the neighbors heard.

I love you, Jack, and your family. You taught me how to be a man, honor my wife, adore my son, and value my adopted country like you do America.

I recovered from nearly drowning, and after a few weeks in a hospital I made my way to every kibbutz Mosha might have reached if she had landed here. I continued searching like the hound dog you knew in Germany and finally found out about a Russian girl who had given birth in a kibbutz outside of Shefalim. I found her! The baby had already been born—it was a miracle that we had all survived. I haven't ever loved anyone or anything as much as I loved Mosha and baby son Yehuda.

I enlisted in the Palmach until we can call ourselves the Army of Israel. Now that you have a new president, Mr. Harry Truman, we are more optimistic.

Keep in touch. We will see each other again someday.
Your loving family,
Mosha, Vladimir, and baby Yehuda

Jack treasured every word of the letter and would reread and translate it in English for the whole family. The bloodline of his deceased brother Yehuda had made a contribution to the future generations of the world.

The second sheet read:

Dear Uncle "Jack":

I will always love you, Uncle Jacov, but I found the love of my life. Papa would be so proud of us. Vladimir is determined to fight for our new homeland, and it is now my home and little Yehuda's too. We are both learning Hebrew and English at the same time. I never want to speak German or Russian again. The next letter, I hope, will be in English.

I tell our son all about his hero uncle and as much as I know about his family. Please send pictures. Something tells me that you will come to visit us before we get to America.

Jack folded the letters neatly, and went into the house yelling, "Bela, Bela, call the family; all of them! Invite them here this evening. Don't take no for an answer. I'm going out to get some champagne."

"What are we celebrating?"

"Vladimir is alive, and Mosha had a baby boy. My oldest brother has been reincarnated. Too bad mama isn't alive to see this. There'd be tears and joy. We are once again a whole family. Tonight we toast the future."

Janet S. Kleinman is a mother, grandmother, and the daughter of immigrants. She is also the author of *Flirting with Disaster when Love and Nature Collide*. In September 2013, she was given a lifetime achievement award from the Brooklyn College Alumni Association. She currently resides in Florida.

Printed in the United States
By Bookmasters